Damien's

Secret II

SUNNI T. CONNOR

DEDICATION

I dedicate this book to my beautiful parents, loving
children, handsome soulmate, and loyal readers.
Thank you all for allowing my imagination to expand,
and for accepting my creativity.

TABLE OF CONTENTS

ACKNOWLEDGMENTS

Published by Naturally Sunni LLC.
Edited by William Hunt

1
BRIANNA'S TURN

Two hard knocks sounded on the door. Brianna's face lit up like a Christmas tree. Dawn frowned and hoped it was Papa or someone that could help. She looked at Brianna, who stood on the side of the door, solid and firm. Brianna cocked the gun back and put her index finger over her perfectly shaped lips to tell Dawn to be quiet. Dawn's heart thumped with anticipation to see who was on the other side of the door. She had never been so scared.

"It's unlocked," Brianna calmly stated. The door opened, and two gunshots were fired.

Dawn's body slowly slid down the sofa, her eyes rolling around uncontrollably, her mouth open as she gasped for air. Her thoughts took over as she lost consciousness.

Now I'm here at this moment. I don't know if I'm dreaming or if I'm dead. I'm in a dark place, and I can't see anything. The sounds are muffled, and I can't seem to find my body parts, but I can still hear my thoughts in my mind. My energy is feeble. I'm trying hard to listen. I'm trying hard to hear Brianna, Damien, or anyone for that matter. But I can't. I can only hear my thoughts. I can't picture anyone's face except my own, which is also Damien's. I can't smell, but I feel a warm sensation, and that gives me hope.

Maybe I'm not dead. Maybe I'm stuck in a nightmare. I'm trying hard to wiggle my toes, but I can't feel them. I can't even see my hand. The warmth I felt seconds ago is gone, and now it feels like a chill. My space is now completely silent. Not even the muffled sounds are here anymore. Where is here? I want to open my eyes, but all I see is darkness. I'm not sure I have eyes anymore.

Damien once told me, "The truth is within the eyes." I want to blink so badly. I want to feel. For the first time ever, I ask God for help. I hate to admit that I'm afraid. I've never felt real fear, and it feels unwelcoming to my body. If I still have a body. I can feel myself leaving wherever I am.

Everything is fading, including my thoughts. I'm fighting for consciousness, but I can feel it drifting away. I'm pretty sure I'm dead now. If I can only blink my eyes, I'll tell the truth about everything. Damien at least deserves the truth before I'm gone forever. His secret is nothing compared to the secret that lives within my death. If the truth is really within the eyes, I can only hope my eyelids will open again. I've now lost my thoughts, and I have nothing left but a blank stare into the deep darkness.

"What the hell is wrong with you?" Craig demanded as he slammed the front door to Dawn's apartment. "Why did you shoot her?" He ran to Dawn's side.

"She deserves to die. She is the scum of the earth!" Brianna paced the room. "What took you so long?" She pulled a rag from her Gucci purse and wiped down the doorknobs.

Craig shook Dawn's limp body, completely ignoring Brianna. "Dawn! Dawn! Can you hear me?"

"No, she can't hear you!" Brianna yelled. "She's dead! Come on, let's go before we both be in jail."

Brianna's words snapped Craig out of his meditative state. "I can't leave her. She is carrying my baby. You lied! You told me you just wanted to talk to her." Craig held Dawn's body in his arms as he rocked back and forth. "Why did you do this, Bella? After all we've been through. Why?" Tears filled his eyes.

"I'll explain later. I promise. But Craig, listen, we have to go." Brianna held Craig's face with both hands and stared into his eyes. "Trust me. You have to leave her."

They both rushed to Craig's car, where they sat in silence. Craig didn't start the vehicle. After two minutes of awkward silence, Brianna suggested they switch seats so she could drive. She turned on the radio and Craig quickly turned it off.

"I need some air," he said, cracking the window. He felt dizzy. His legs were numb, and his heart ached. He had grown to love Dawn, and he was excited to meet his unborn child. He knew Dawn was the last woman he would ever be with intimately, and he knew their baby was the only baby he would create out of love. If he ever had a baby with another man, it would have to be some stranger sergeant mom.

As Brianna drove them away from Dawn's apartment, Craig hung his head. "Where are we even going?"

"To the cabin. I know you can't see this right now, but this is a good thing, Craig."

"Good thing? Bella, are you fucking nuts? You just murdered the woman I loved, and she was carrying my child. I don't even know why I'm still in this car with you." Craig punched the dashboard, causing the compartment to pop open and spill napkins to the floor.

"I thought you loved Damien? You couldn't

possibly love Dawn—she's evil. Well, she *was* evil—not that you really knew her."

"And you did? You've been in hiding for the last ten years, but I've been with her for years. I think I know who she was."

"Oh, I know her, alright," Brianna said ominously.

"What's that supposed to mean?"

"Let's just talk when we get to the cabin. Right now we need to focus on leaving the city—and getting you a solid alibi.

"Why would I need an alibi? Is there something else you need to tell me?" Craig stared hard at Brianna's face, suspicious she wasn't telling him everything.

"No, Craig. It's just—you were her fiancé, which makes you the most obvious suspect. I really shouldn't have told you to meet me there, but it was the only way I could get her address from you. That was my biggest mistake. What if someone saw you?" Her eyes glazed over as she stared at the road, as if she had fallen deep in a daydream.

"I don't care if anyone saw me. I didn't do anything! You're the one who planned this all out. Who are you, anyway?"

"I'm your sister, Bella. Nothing has changed." Her hand shook on the steering wheel. "You have to trust me. I will protect you at all costs. You protected me once, and now it's time I return the favor."

"I can do without your favors," he mumbled under his breath.

She stared into Craig's eyes, glancing occasionally back at the road. "Dawn was not who you thought she was, and I know you are hurting right now, but I would shoot her again. I would do anything to protect us."

Craig looked away. "I don't want to talk about this anymore."

The turn signal clicked like a metronome as they pulled onto the long road leading to the cabin. Craig had his seat belt off and his hand on the door handle before the tires had stopped crunching the gravel.

As Craig stepped into the familiar driveway and smelled the fresh scent of pines, he felt his body relax for the first time since meeting up with Brianna. The cabin had long been a safe place for them both. Craig's adoptive parents owned the cabin, and his family went there every weekend. It was tucked away from the road, offering privacy and peace of mind. Nobody would bother them here.

Instead of going inside with Brianna, Craig decided to sit on the wooden porch in a hammock. He found himself lost in deep thought. He swung in the hammock, recalling the day he had met Brianna. It seemed like the working of fate now.

Shortly after hearing the news from his adoptive parents that his biological father, Ralph, had been murdered, Craig decided to return to his old house to retrieve a very special picture and bracelet of his mother's. He was thirteen at the time.

Craig hated Ralph's house, which held so many bad memories, especially the basement. That was where his father had kept him locked up for months after realizing he was gay. It was also where his father had raped him. Craig had every intention of sneaking into the house, which was still encircled in yellow caution tape like a terrible gift wrapped just for him, grabbing the few sacred belongings, and running out without staying a second longer than necessary.

When he entered the cold, vacant, and dark house, however, he felt a complicated ball of emotions. Everything came crashing down on him. He turned on his flashlight, and his heart thumped at each creaking step. The house carried an echo and smelled of death.

First he went to his old room and looked at all his raggedy old thrift-store toys. He picked up an old baseball his uncle had given him years ago and threw it into his backpack. He walked down the hallway and snatched a picture of his mother off the wall. He continued to Ralph's room, which hadn't been cleaned since his murder.

Craig entered the room with caution. Blood was splattered on everything, including the cream-colored sheets, which had turned brown with old blood. Craig was only there a few seconds before he felt a compulsive need to rush back to the hallway.

Taking deep breaths to compose himself, Craig told himself there was nothing to be afraid of. He slowly walked back into the disturbing room and immediately looked for the chest that held his mother's belongings. He felt a surge of relief when he found the bracelet and the photo of him and his mom on the beach. It was just the two of them in the old polaroid picture, his mother holding him tight as her big beach hat fell over her face. Craig smiled, rubbing the picture tenderly with his thumb.

As he slipped the picture into his bag, he heard someone walking around the house. He stood still to listen, shaking uncontrollably with fear.

Not wanting to run into any robbers or criminals, Craig scrambled under the bloody bed his father had been murdered in and waited. He prayed whoever was in the house wouldn't come upstairs. It felt like he was under the bed for an eternity. He closed his eyes at the sound of footsteps coming up the stairs, so terrified that he urinated himself. Suddenly, the footsteps retreated back down the stairs and into the basement. Shortly after, a door slammed.

Craig impatiently waited another five minutes before moving. As he rolled out from under the bed, the acrid scent of smoke tickled his nose. Panicking, he snatched his bag and ran down the steps even as the smoke thickened and the flames roared. But the fire hadn't made its way upstairs yet, and this gave him hope he might still escape.

The flames were already licking at the front door, so he raced to the back door. Just as he touched the doorknob, however, someone started coughing. The sound was coming from the basement, the place Craig feared more than any other. He considered rushing out of the house, but his curiosity wouldn't allow him to leave someone to burn to death.

"Hello!" he whispered with fear, coughing as he opened the basement door. "Is someone down there?"

"Help, please help!" a faint voice responded, weak and frail.

"I'm coming!" Craig screamed as he jumped down the basement steps two at a time. His heart raced with anxiety and fear.

"I'm over here." Brianna's words were punctuated with coughs. "I can't move."

"What happened to you? The house is burning down fast. Can you try to walk?" Craig tried to lift Brianna from the cold concrete floor, but she spilled from his grasp like a limp fish.

"I can't. Just leave me. Save yourself. Just tell my family it was…." Brianna's head rolled back before she could finish. She was unconscious but still breathing.

"I'll get you out of here," Craig whispered as he struggled to drag Brianna's body up the basement steps. After making it halfway up the steps he realized she was too heavy for his scrawny thirteen year old body. He let her go and ran to the top of the steps.

Before he opened the basement door, he glanced at Brianna who was hunched over, motionless. "I can't leave her, she'll die," he mumbled to himself before running back down the steps to pull her up with all his might.

The smoke was getting thicker and the mission seemed more impossible with each step he took. Without realizing it, Craig had made it to the back door. He dragged Brianna down the three outside steps. Coughing uncontrollably, he fell to the grass, gasping for air.

"Hey! Wake up," he demanded, while shaking Brianna.

She didn't respond, but he saw her arm move so he knew she was alive. He panicked and ran to the payphone to call his adoptive parents. They frantically asked a million questions and then promised to be there right away. Craig and Brianna waited in the backyard of a vacant house two doors down from the fire.

While waiting, Craig reminisced on the few fun times he'd had in that house while his mother was alive. His thoughts quickly changed as he watched the gray smoke fill the air. He was afraid to call the police because he thought he would be blamed for the fire, or maybe someone would discover Ralph was his father. He never wanted anyone to know that. He had no idea what to do with Brianna. He decided the police would find her and he could just leave with his family when they arrived.

Brianna began to look around with weak faint eyes.

"I'm glad you woke back up," Craig said. "The police will find you here. Just yell when they come to put out the fire."

"Water!" Brianna begged in a low tone. Craig took a water bottle from his backpack, unscrewed the cap, and pressed the bottle to Brianna's lips as if she were a baby. She drank fast.

"What's your name?" Craig asked. "What were you doing in there?"

"Please take me with you. She will find me and finish killing me. She's a maniac!" She fell into a coughing fit, unable to say more.

"Who? Who will find you? I can't take you with me. My parents will never go for it."

"My parents are sex attics, and I was their sex slave. Don't make me go back there. Just tell your parents. I promise not to be a fuss. I'll stay out of everyone's way. It's better if she thinks I'm dead." Brianna's eyes were round and hollow with dread.

Craig frowned, confused. "Who? Your mother?"

"No, the devil. She's real. I'm scared to say her name because she may know I'm alive and haunt me in my dreams. She's the one who burned the house down. She tried to burn me up with it. She thought she had already killed me, and she came to finish the job. I've been in that basement for I don't know how long. I guess I've been unconscious. I only remember waking up when I smelled the smoke."

"That sounds terrible, but this is too much. We can't just keep you. I'm sure people are looking for you—they'll help you."

"The only one who'll be looking for me is *her*. You might as well have left me in that fire to die. She'll kill me if she finds me here—I'm sure of it. She's a cold-blooded monster. You are my only chance at a normal life." She swallowed hard, steadying herself. "My name is Brianna, by the way."

"I'm Craig. Crap, there goes my parents." Craig stood up to wave his parents down.

"Tell them my family is trying to kill me, please. Tell them anything you have to."

"I'll try," Craig whispered before he walked to his parents' brand new Lincoln Town Car and opened the door.

"Hurry up, get in!" his adoptive father said. "What happened? What are you doing here?"

"It's a long story, Dad, and I don't have time to explain now, but I can't get in the car without that girl." He pointed at Brianna.

"You better get in this damn car," his adoptive mother demanded. "I mean right now, Craig!"

"I'm sorry, but I can't leave her. Her parents tried to kill her tonight, and her father rapes her. I saved her from the fire. If I leave her, then we will all be responsible for her death."

All three turned their heads at the wail of approaching sirens.

"Hurry up and get in the car!" his mother said. "Your father just signed the biggest deal of his career, it's hard enough for a black man. You know he can't be in the media spotlight right now."

"I'm sorry, Mom. I can't leave her. They tried to burn her alive tonight, and if I leave her, they'll come back to finish the job. I just can't do it." Craig fidgeted with the zipper on his jacket to avoid his parents' eyes. "What if you both never saved me? I have the chance to save her. Either she comes, or I can't come home. I love you both, but I can't leave her." His voice had grown husky with tears.

Craig's mother softened as she looked at Brianna. "How about we take her with us tonight? Then we can talk again in the morning and decide what to do."

"Help me with her, Dad," Craig urged, knowing the cops would arrive at any moment. "She can't walk."

Craig and his dad helped Brianna into the car and drove off, passing several policemen and fire trucks screaming down the road.

When they reached Craig's parents' house, Brianna showed them the scratches and bruises Dawn had left on her neck. She lied, telling them the marks had come from her mother and she was her parents' sex slave. She convinced them her parents would find her if they knew she was alive. Neither foster care nor the police could keep her safe. Craig's adoptive parents had always had a weak spot for abused children—it was why they had adopted Craig.

That night, after hearing Brianna's horror stories, they all decided to keep her. They renamed her **Bella** and decided that, to protect her from being found by her abusive parents, they would homeschool her and only let her leave the house on weekends to stay at the cabin—the one place outside the house where she was safe from the risk of being recognized.

Now, ten years after the fire, Craig was in shock that the girl he had rescued from that basement had murdered Dawn and his unborn child. He didn't want to be around Brianna anymore–or anyone else, for that matter. He needed time to process everything that had happened.

A few hours passed before Brianna came to the front door, carrying two cups of coffee.

"Are you ready to talk now?" she asked, handing Craig a cup.

"Only if you are ready to tell me what is really going on," Craig barked as he snatched the cup, spilling coffee on his hand.

"Come inside, and I'll tell you everything. I'll tell you the real truth about the night you found me." Brianna held the door open, inviting him.

"I was just thinking about that night," Craig admitted as he stepped through the doorway. "I'm questioning everything I thought I knew about you. I love you more than anything, but right now, I don't even know who you are." He sat near the fire and gazed into the flames.

"I never wanted to talk about this—I wanted to protect you. But I owe you the truth after what happened today." Brianna sighed heavily. "Dawn is the one who tried to kill me that night. She's the devil

I was talking about. She's possessed."

Craig raised his eyebrows. "Dawn is the mysterious person you've been calling the devil all these years? Why would she try to kill you?" He watched her closely, trying to understand.

Brianna kept her voice low, as if fearing Dawn might overhear her. "She was a control freak. She seemed so perfect and innocent, but she was really demonic. She planted nightmares in my mind to make me be her friend."

"This sounds crazy! I was with Dawn for years, and I never detected an ounce of evil in her."

"I understand this may be hard to believe, but she was manipulative. She could play whatever character she wanted. She haunted me with nightmares, which is why I was so afraid that she would kill me if she knew I was still alive. It was me or her, Craig."

"She was only thirteen, Bella. You could've gotten her arrested, sent to juvie."

"It wasn't that simple. Dawn controlled my mind. The nightmares only stopped when she thought I was dead. Can you imagine sleeping in terror every single night of your life? She used my deepest fears to scare me."

"What about your parents? Did you lie about them, too?" Craig's voice dripped with sarcasm—he felt hurt that she had lied to him for so long.

"Yes." Brianna lowered her head in shame. "My parents were the most amazing people, and they spoiled and loved me like no other. I was their only child. Their hearts must have broken into pieces, thinking of me, missing me, wondering what happened to me. My poor mother." Brianna covered her mouth to still her trembling lips.

"Okay, let me get this straight. You're saying Dawn strangled you and tried to burn you up the day I went to get my mother's picture from my dad's house?" He looked directly at Brianna. "Your parents aren't really into sex slaving or whatever, but you said they were. You said all of that so Dawn would think you were dead?"

"Yes. Except for the day of the fire, she thought I was dead already. I lay in the basement for days, too weak to yell for help or crawl up the steps. I was in and out of consciousness, and I just lay there, unable to get the strength to leave." Tears filled her eyes. "Then she came back to burn the house down, to get rid of me for good. I've missed my parents so much, and now that she is dead, I know she can't haunt me, and I know my parents will be safe. Now I can go find them. Thank you for all you've done for me over the years. You are truly my brother." She moved closer to Craig.

"But you still haven't told me why she tried to kill you in the first place."

"I can't tell you why. It has something to do with Dawn's twin brother, Damien. You won't like it. I know you love Damien, so for now, that's all I can tell you."

"Well, that's some bullshit. I appreciate you opening up—halfway! But I can't just forgive you right away. I need some time, Bella. I do love you like a real sister, but this is a lot to take in. I've just seen my girlfriend murdered, along with our baby."

"I understand. I hope you can forgive me one day." Brianna lowered her head. She grabbed the remote and turned the television to the news station to change the subject.

Today in Detroit, we had a fire on Woodward Avenue. There were two casualties. Sadly, gunshots were reported on the other side of town, and a twenty-three-year-old woman was found. The police have not released her identity or her condition. They are asking anyone with information to contact the Detroit police department, as this is an active investigation.

In other news, a lady found a cat stuck in a tree with three new kittens...

"What the hell?" Brianna exclaimed. "Why didn't they say if she was dead or not?" She turned off the TV and began pacing back and forth.

"She's dead. She didn't have a pulse. They never like to give too much information, so the killer will be left in the dark. How does it feel, being in the dark?"

"Craig, this is not the time for your sarcastic remarks. What if she survived somehow? Now she knows I'm alive. I should've shot that piece of trash again. Fuck!"

2
PAPA'S HERE

"Girl, why you got your door wide open?" Papa yelled as he walked into Dawn's apartment. "Oh my God, Dawn! Get up! Get up! Come on, baby girl." He opened Dawn's eyelids and felt her wrist. "Who did this to you? Dawn, please. Come on, get up!" He shook Dawn as he dialed 9-1-1.

"Nine-one-one, what's your emergency?" the operator asked.

"My daughter was shot. She's not responding. I can't feel a pulse."

"Calm down, sir. Are you safe? Where are you?"

"Parks Place Apartments on…" Papa stopped mid-sentence and looked at Dawn with pity.

"Someone close by called in the gunshots, and the ambulance is already on its way. Don't move the victim, okay?"

Papa dropped the phone. "Dawn, get up! Come on, baby. I need you. If you can hear me in there, stay with me. It'll be okay. I'm here now. Papa's here now. Come on, Dawn, hold on." He talked to Dawn's unresponsive body as tears filled his eyes.

The medics put Dawn's limp body on a stretcher. Papa wiped tears from his eyes as he climbed into the ambulance with Dawn. They pumped Dawn's body over and over but could not restart her heart. Papa lowered his head and prayed. When he lifted his head back up, the paramedics told him he had to move back while they worked on Dawn. *"Work on Dawn?"* his mind raced as thoughts of Dawn took over his body.

Papa had always loved Dawn. She was the child he had hoped for. In his eyes, she was absolutely perfect. He had been late to her birth, sure, but he had been so excited to hold a mini version of Mama in his arms. Dawn had all of Mama's beautiful features.

Then Papa thought of Damien. Poor Damien. When Mama was pregnant, they both wanted a girl. Papa thought girls were unique because they could carry life. He wanted something precious and innocent to love forever. He wanted a girl version of Mama to call his own, and Dawn met all his expectations. Damien, however, did not. Not only was Damien unexpected, but he was also a boy. Papa would've preferred twin girls if it had to be two babies.

As the paramedics worked on Dawn, Papa's thoughts fell into an old memory of Dawn. She was five years old, and that Christmas, Papa bought Dawn and Damien a bike. He was only interested in teaching Dawn how to ride, but he knew he would be forced to show Damien, too. They were outside their Detroit home, and Damien was begging to learn first. Dawn didn't care about the order, but Papa refused to show Damien first.

He remembered how he held Dawn up on her bike and slowly walked with her while Damien, trying to learn to ride by himself, fell repeatedly. Papa became annoyed with Damien as he cried from hurting himself on his last fall. Papa had to stop helping Dawn and take Damien to the house with his busted knee. That was the part Papa remembered the most—having to stop his time with Dawn to help the unwanted Damien.

Papa's love for Damien changed that day. Surprisingly, he finally started loving him. Not because he hurt himself, but because Dawn loved him. A few hours later, when Papa came outside to get them both for dinner, Dawn was holding Damien's bike up, and she had taught him everything

Papa had taught her.

Papa observed Dawn letting go of Damien's bike, and how Damien rode on his own for the very first time. Dawn immediately grabbed her bike, and they rode together. That was when Papa knew they came as a pair, and no matter how much he preferred Dawn, Damien would always be there waiting to learn how to ride too.

Papa's thoughts were interrupted as the ambulance came to an abrupt stop. He looked up at Dawn's lifeless body as the paramedics pulled the stretcher off the ambulance.

"We have an African American female, age twenty-three, with two gunshot wounds, one to the head and one to the chest," the paramedic told the hospital staff as they rushed Dawn down the hall, calling her name. "She was found by her father. Her pulse is weak, and we've been working on her the entire ride. She lost a lot of blood, which her father said is O-type."

"Sir, please step back," the doctor told Papa as several of the orderlies restrained him. "We will take it from here."

"That's my daughter! My daughter! I want to go with her!"

One of the nurses paused to assure Papa while the rest of the staff hurried Dawn down the hall. "I understand, sir. We will do our best to save her, but you have to let us do our job. Soon as we know something, we'll let you know."

Papa felt lost, and all he wanted was to be with Mama. He wanted to hug her as they cried about their precious baby girl. Papa sat in the waiting area, shaking his leg and wondering where Mama had gone. He thought of her moving on with another man. He couldn't understand why he couldn't reach her. Even when Mama had left Aunt Sheryl's house, she had still come to see Papa and never missed one visit. Weirdly enough, though, she had lost all contact before Papa's trial, which never sat right with Papa. Mama had been so excited about the re-trial—he couldn't believe it when she didn't show up to one single appearance.

Papa was exhausted from crying and waiting. No one had told him anything about Dawn's condition, and every time he asked, they told him just to be patient. Papa walked to the vending machine, inserted two wrinkled-up dollars, and chose a bottle of water. When it got stuck on its way down, Papa started punching and shaking the machine uncontrollably. He screamed and yelled as security pulled him back.

He sat back down and waited as the detectives came to ask him the same questions the previous detectives had asked.

One hour later, the doctor joined Papa in the waiting room.

"Mr. Scott. I'm Dr. Smidget. I wish we were meeting on better terms. We were able to bring Dawn back, but she's in a comatose state. She has a weak pulse, and the machines are keeping her alive at this point."

He jumped to his feet. "Oh my God, thank you for bringing her back. That's my baby. That's my baby girl!"

"I won't lie to you. We don't know if Dawn will make it. She's been through a lot. Not too long ago, she came out of a coma caused by another incident. We are hopeful she'll pull through again, though."

"I never go to Dawn's house so late, but since her mother went missing I worry a lot. When I tried to call Dawn, she didn't answer, and she always answered me. I'm glad I went. I know this is a lot to be telling you, doc. I'm sorry. I'm all over the place. Thank you for saving my baby and I know she'll wake up. Thank you." Papa reached out to grab the doctor's hand.

"It's okay, Mr. Scott. Don't thank me yet. Thank me when Dawn is breathing for herself again. She's a beautiful girl, and we are all praying she pulls through. You can see her for five minutes, and then we have to let her rest."

Papa walked into Dawn's cold, all-white hospital room in the intensive care unit. He grabbed Dawn's hand, which was small and frail compared to his manly one. He admired her fresh manicure, and he noticed how her hands favored Mama's hands. Her head was bandaged up, her face swollen and tired. She didn't look strong—she hardly looked like she was even inside her own body. Papa couldn't feel her presence, and he felt like he was staring at Dawn in a coffin. She had lost life, and it broke his heart. He knew the doctor had saved a dead girl. He knew Dawn would never be the same, and it was a hard pill to swallow. It was too painful to see Dawn that way. The least he could do was find out who did this to her. Find out who tried to take the life of a life he had created.

Papa's phone rang as he stood up to leave Dawn's room. The number was blocked.

"Hello!" Papa answered.

"Is she alive?" The voice sounded robotic, as if deliberately distorted to hide the speaker's identity.

"Who is this?"

"First tell me if she's alive."

"I'm not playing these games with you—whoever you are!"

"Your daughter is a maniac, a serial killer, and your son is a sick anal freak!"

Papa felt his face turning red with rage. "My daughter is fighting for her life, and you have the balls to call and threaten *me*? I will take my bare hands and wring your fucking neck!"

"You won't do anything Jerome. You are stupid and don't even know your own children. Will you wring my neck like Dawn did? Did she learn how to wring people's necks from you?"

"What? Dawn wouldn't hurt anyone. Who are you?" With a deep breath, Papa calmed himself. The angrier he got, the less information he was likely to get, and he needed to know who had tried to kill Dawn.

"You're delusional. Dawn is a murderer. Have you had any nightmares lately? Do you ever wonder why they stopped?"

"Fuck you!" Papa shouted, losing his patience again. His nightmares were a sensitive subject, and he had only told his brother Robby and Mama. Robby was mentally gone, and Mama wouldn't want Dawn dead, so how did this person know about his nightmares?

"I bet you look confused right now. Don't be. I'll clear everything up for you, really soon."

An awkward silence took over the phone.

"You still there? I'll find you!" he yelled.

"I've been lost for years, and if someone finds me,

it won't be you. You could do the world a favor, though, and finish Dawn off. You created that monster, so you should take her out!"

"What the hell are you talking about? Dawn is no monster. Hello? Hello?"

Without warning, the line had disconnected.

3
JAIL

I slowly opened my eyes, smelled the repugnant odor of rat feces and urine, and groaned as I realized I was exactly where I dreaded to be: stuck in a box with four white walls.

Every morning, like clockwork, I woke to the guards yelling and talking trash. I hadn't heard anything from the outside world, yet another reminder of how alone I was.

After being arrested three days earlier, the guards provided me with one phone call. Sadly, I had no one to call. I wanted to call Craig, but I was upset he hadn't left the money he'd promised. I wouldn't have ended up in prison if I hadn't had to search Dawn's place high and low for the money. Thanks to Craig, I ran right into Detective Ross's handcuffs.

I was constantly worried that someone would see my weakness. For years I had hidden my sexuality to avoid the condemnation of my family, and still, I had to hide. I thought if everyone knew I was gay, it would feel like freedom. I imagined freedom would feel like living without judgment. I thought individualism would allow me to live my life MY WAY. I wanted to cut the imaginary rope I thought society had hung around my neck with their expectations. It was always my life, not theirs. My sexuality was always a choice, but not in prison. In prison I had to be smart, which meant I had to keep pretending.

Although I was attracted to men, I had no intentions of becoming someone's bitch or getting gang-raped. So after all the crap I had done to hide being gay, I was still imprisoned and still had to pretend I was into women. The other inmates were violent scavengers who wanted either blood or somebody's ass. I wasn't willing to give up either. No one knew me, and I wasn't repping any neighborhood or gang. My plan was to stay quiet, but I knew that wouldn't work forever. Papa punishing me with a black eye that hadn't fully healed didn't really help my prison image.

The inmates wore all-white uniforms. It was ridiculous. Why would they make us wear white? Were we supposed to be a bunch of choir boys? You could tell the inmates who had been arrested the longest, by the dingy color of their jail suits.

They only gave me one toothbrush, a thin blanket, and a piece of cotton they called a mattress. My one bar of soap was already too thin to properly coat the rag I used for showering. If I couldn't wash up, I'd just die. The thought of running out of toothpaste was just too scary to imagine. Everyone knew I was a neat freak. I loved to smell good, and I loved brushing my teeth. They said I could order from the store, but I didn't have any money on my books. Look at me, already knowing this jail talk.

"Open C Block six!" yelled a correctional officer named David. He looked at me and smiled as if he knew something I didn't. "Okay, you little shit turds. It's time to get up!"

David was a fraud. I could tell he was the type of kid who got bullied when he was younger, so he decided to grow some balls and get a job to bully other people. What a fucked-up world we live in.

I got on David's bad side the first day I got booked. I refused to talk to him, and I ignored his questions during the intake process. I was furious the day I was arrested, and silence was my friend. It wasn't a good idea to ignore David, though, as I later realized when he started making things extremely difficult for me.

David put me in a cell with this young guy named Crazy Joe. He never told me his real name, but he was indeed mentally disturbed. Crazy Joe was a short, stocky guy. He was only about five feet, and he wore two old frizzy braids that seemed to have been in his hair forever. Crazy Joe annoyingly paced the cell all day. He never sat down. He talked aloud about how he was going to kill "these motherfuckas," whoever they were. He screamed and talked all night.

As if sharing a cell with Crazy Joe wasn't enough, I also had to avoid going out into the general population for fear I'd be exposed. I worried I'd kill someone and never get out, or perhaps I'd get raped. Frankly, I was terrified every second I was in that hell hole.

Crazy Joe was starting to drive me crazy. It was time for me to get out of the cell. We were only allowed out of the cell for two hours each day. When I came from breakfast, I made my mind up that I would finally leave the cell.

I had been arrested for Mr. Ralph's murder and Brianna's disappearance. There was no way I was getting out anytime soon, so it was time to stop hiding.

My cellmate took a shit every morning after breakfast. It was the most degrading part about being in jail. Who actually wants to smell someone's feces? Especially someone who never shuts the fuck up.

"Yoooo, what the hell?' Crazy Joe asked. "Your scary-ass leaving the cell?"

"Yeah, I'm going to rec," I replied as I brushed my teeth.

"Hell no! You got me fucked up! If you leave, they leave. You feel me?" His words were punctuated by plops of water as his crap splashed into the toilet.

"Who leaves?" I asked in a confused tone. I was curious to know if that was some type of slang that I should know about.

"Them motherfuckas! See, you got shit fucked up! This ain't your world. Shit that goes up must come down unless the shit comes out. You feel me?" He farted and grabbed a handful of toilet paper.

"Nah, I don't feel you," I said as I looked for my book so I could hurry up and leave the foul-smelling cell.

"Don't shit come out of your ass? Or do you think you too good? I smelled your stinking ass. You always try to hold it until you think I'm asleep. I still be smelling your stinking ass." His voice rose to a sing-song tone. "Damien's ass stinks, Damien's ass stinks, just likc mincs, just likc mincs."

"Have you seen my book?" I asked, disregarding his insults while holding my nose. It was humiliating enough to use the bathroom when someone else was in my space. I definitely didn't want to discuss bowel movements with some nut job.

"Yeah, I saw it. I ate that motherfucka!" Crazy Joe laughed uncontrollably before going into a rant about how we were living on a foreign planet. I chose to leave the cell without the damn book because it wasn't worth the conversation or the smell.

Before I stepped all the way out, however, I looked to my left and then my right. My heart thumped with anxiety as I listened to the jail chatter. It was a loud combination of multiple conversations. I had no idea where to go. To the left was the Skinhead crew, but to the right were the Blacks and Mexicans. Some of the black people were Muslims, and some were in gangs with tattoos on their necks. There was a group of older guys playing cards, but even they seemed to be a crew.

I walked toward the right. I was pretty sure I didn't have a place on the left with the white supremacists. Every step I took was heavy. It felt like I had ten pounds of sand in my shoes. The prison was freezing cold, but I had to act like it was nothing. I couldn't be walking around shivering like a little bitch. I also had to remember to walk hard. I knew how to do that well from all the years of faking my masculinity.

"Look who's finally out of the cell!" David, the correctional officer, yelled loud enough for everyone to hear. Suddenly all eyes were on me. I remembered being younger and craving attention, stomping in the classroom so everyone could see me, and now I wished for nothing less.

I ignored David and the other COs, who were laughing right along with him. The problem was I didn't know where to walk. Who to sit with? I decided to walk over to the old heads. They reminded me of the old guys from my childhood neighborhood who played the lottery and talked trash about politics.

"This table is closed, young buck. We only have two decks of cards, and our games are full." The older man said, never looking up from the cards in his hands.

"Ard, cool, thanks," I answered awkwardly.

"Ard, cool? Where you from?" a guy named Big Mike asked, who sat on the table instead of the chair. Calling him "Big Mike" was an understatement—the dude was enormous.

"I'm from around," I casually responded.

"Oh, ard," Big Mike said. "Being from around ain't nowhcrc up in hcrc. So you might want to go back to your cell."

"Nah, I'm good," I replied as I wandered the room for my next destination.

"That wasn't a request. You feel me? I'm Big Mike, so now you know. I run shit over here. So until you figure out where you from, then you have nowhere to go."

Everyone looked at me to see what I would do. I knew if I walked back to the cell, I would never get respect or be able to come back out.

"Wassup, Big Mike," I greeted him as if we had just met. "I understand that wasn't a request from you, but I wasn't asking." My heart was beating so loud, I was surprised the ground didn't shake.

Big Mike grinned at the guy beside him. "New fools always love to learn by example, don't they?"

I had begun walking away when suddenly I felt a painful sting as a chair crashed into me from behind, knocking me to the floor. I quickly got up and put my hands in a fighting position. I swung at Big Mike, but I missed. I heard the wind coming before his punch, and I ducked just in time. I swiftly slung another blow, and that time I hit him.

Then one of his boys hit me. The inmates circled us, and all I could hear was the commotion. Then something in me snapped. I realized who I was. I wasn't someone to be fucked with. I was Damien.

Suddenly, Dawn's face appeared in my head. I channeled the same anger that had caused me to throw her over a mountain, and I squared up.

We went blow for blow. I fought all three men, and I don't know where I got the strength to stay up as long as I did. Someone hit me in the head with something, and I finally crashed to the floor. I knew the bottom was the worst place to be in a fight, but I couldn't get up fast enough.

As my attackers stomped me, I balled up in a fetal position. Mama's voice popped into my head, cutting through the chaos of pain. I'd heard her voice before when I found myself in challenging situations, but her voice seemed so far away this time.

"You better get your ass up!" she screamed in my mind.

I bit one of the guy's ankles so hard a chunk of blood and skin came free in my mouth. He hollered like a night wolf.

I pulled one of the other guys to the floor with me, and we rolled around for a second before he ran out of energy. Finally, it was just Big Mike and me. When the other two tried to charge me again, the crowd held them back. Big Mike and I went blow for blow; just when I didn't have an ounce of energy left, the guards hit Big Mike and me with batons. We both fell to the floor on our stomachs with our arms flat in a surrender position. Big Mike won the fight, but I

gained enough respect to come back out of the cell—
which was precisely what I planned to do.

It wasn't long before they were dragging me to the
medical unit. Apparently, Big Mike had whipped my
ass more than I thought. They bandaged my head,
gave me two Motrins, and sent me back to the cell.

As I walked through the tier with the correctional
officers, a few prisoners nodded at me and I nodded
back. I now felt like I had somewhere to sit. That
fight gave me respect. As soon as I walked into the
cell, Crazy Joe had a lot to say. I was two seconds
from punching him in the throat, but I knew my
body was too weak for another fight on the same
day, so I reluctantly let him talk as he paced the cell.

"I told your dumb ass if you leave, they leave. But
you wouldn't listen."

"What the fuck does that mean, Joe?" I asked.

"Hey, hey, hey! Don't come back in here like you
Mike Tyson, or something. I will still kick your scary
ass. Like I told you, what comes up must come
down!"

"Okay, Joe."

"No, it's not okay, and it's not Joe. It's Crazy Joe!
That's the sixth time today you called me Joe. That
ain't my name!"

I decided to go along just to shut him up. "Look,
I'm just tired. My bad, Crazy Joe."

Crazy Joe began urinating while he talked. He was
not very accurate with his aim.

"I know you tired, cause big man whipped your ass. When they come back, don't think I'm a help you. I told you when you leave, they leave. But did you listen? No! You wanted to be curious and dumb, just like the other newbies."

"What do you mean, when they come back?"

"Are you listening, Dum-Dum? Sometimes talking to you is like talking to a brick wall. Yeah, they are coming back! Do you think you only have to fight once in prison? Furthermore, how do you think we got on this foreign planet in the first place? You don't think they are coming?" His face was dead serious as if he believed every word he was saying.

"I don't know, Joe—Crazy Joe, I mean."

Talking to him was becoming more and more exhausting. I jumped on the top bunk, which confirmed how sore my body was. I thought about "them" coming back, but Crazy Joe was all over the place and usually made no sense. I would have to deal with that if and when it happened.

All I could think of was Mama. I knew she would hate me if she learned what I had done to Dawn.

Just as I dozed off, they called us for our three o'clock dinner. I debated whether to go to dinner in my condition and risk another beatdown.

In the end, I decided I was too hungry not to go. I tried not to limp as I walked to the cafeteria, but it was obvious I wasn't feeling one hundred. Besides, everyone saw what happened to me, so who was I trying to fool?

I grabbed my tray and sat down. To my surprise, I was able to eat in peace. I heard a few slick remarks, but nothing I couldn't block out. Some guys even seemed to have more respect for me, while others laughed at me. I felt someone keep looking in my direction as I ate. Eventually I caught him looking and made eye contact, and we stared at one another for a moment before he looked down. He seemed very familiar, but I couldn't pinpoint why.

"Yo, do you know that guy?" I asked Matt. He was another new guy who sat across from me, serving time for drug possession and distribution. Matt was a tall and slinky white guy who had red spots all over his face. We had gotten booked on the same day. He was the only other person I talked to besides Crazy Joe.

"Naw, I don't know him, but I heard some guys talking about why he was in here," Matt whispered.

"What is in here for?" I questioned as I took a bite of my bread roll.

Matt frowned at me as if I was talking too loud.

I lowered my voice to a whisper. "My bad, yo. He just looks familiar."

"Child pornography is what I heard. I wasn't

going to ask what happened to you, but are you okay?"

"Yeah, I'm good. I just decided to leave my cell. Crazy Joe told me, 'What comes up must come down,' whatever the fuck that means." I laughed.

"Damien, you a fool. Shit, I ain't tryna look like you. I guess I better keep my ass in my cell then." He laughed, too.

"So he was arrested for messing with kids? I know I have seen him before."

I ate a spoonful of cold, tasteless mashed potatoes. Every time I ate them, I missed Mama's cooking because she made the best buttery mashed potatoes ever.

"Yeah, that's what I heard. Little boys, they said. They planning on getting him in the showers later. I hear stuff, but I just keep quiet, you know. Dude, this jail shit is hard. I've been sick from kicking the dope. They don't give you shit to feel better, not even a Motrin. I've just been ill. Dude, when I get out, I'm leaving that drug shit alone."

"Yeah, I hope you do. Shit, I can't even think about getting out. With my charges, I'll be in here forever." My head instinctively sank, but then I remembered where I was and straightened again. I couldn't afford to show weakness, not even in the way I held my head.

While talking with Matt, I suddenly remembered who the man was. It was my middle school principal, Mr. Lewis. I couldn't believe he had been arrested for messing with little boys. No wonder he had loved keeping us in detention when I was in school. As I thought about it, I realized I had never seen a girl in detention with us boys.

Mr. Lewis looked so different now. He was much darker and fatter. His nose still covered his entire face, but he was hard to recognize, especially after so many years. He apparently had no trouble recognizing me, though. If he had been messing with children, he would get just what he deserved.

Dinner was over, so I got up to throw my tray in the tray bin. I saw Big Mike and two other dudes walking toward me. I prepared myself to fight again, but David, the correctional officer, called my name to see the counselor before they could reach me. I wondered why I had to see the counselor again so soon. Maybe I had to speak with her because of the fight. Either way, I was relieved David came to get me before Big Mike could.

"Hi, Damien. How are you adjusting?" Emma, the prison counselor, wore a pencil skirt and a white blouse. She was bland and pale almost like a white woman, nothing special. Her face was slim, mediocre, unimpressive—a face I would quickly forget on the streets.

"I'm okay. Been better."

She studied her notepad. "Well, I heard you got into a fight today. Do you feel threatened, or like your life is in danger?"

I glanced at David, who stood guard at the door with his arms crossed. "Nah, I'm good."

"Officer David, you can leave us. I feel safe. I'll let you know if I need anything."

"Emma, with all due respect. I don't think you should be alone with this inmate, based on his charges."

"I got it. I can handle myself, and you'll be right outside the door. Plus, Damien looks pretty hurt; I think I can take him," she joked.

"Alright, it's your call. I'll be outside the door." David glared at me. "Don't you try nothing stupid."

Emma waited until David had shut the door. Then she leaned toward me and spoke in a low voice.

"Now that we are alone, I have a message for you. I could lose my job for this, so I hope you keep this confidential. My brother-in-law asked for a favor, so I'm trusting this message is vital for one of his patients."

"A message? From who?"

"He said — I can't give you his name — he said Dawn was found in the mountains half-dead, but she is alive and doing better. She hit her head pretty hard, and now she has amnesia. She doesn't even remember her name. He couldn't provide any other medical diagnosis because of HIPAA, but she wants you to call or come see her. The doctor thinks it will help her regain her memory."

"For real? That's great. Are you sure it's Dawn? She really has amnesia?"

Emma raised her eyebrows. "You don't seem shocked. If my sister fell off a mountain, I would be appalled. Did you know about her accident?"

"No, I didn't know. I just said it's great that Dawn's okay. Who survives a mountain fall?" I shook my head, as if marveling. "So you said the accident caused her to forget everything?"

Emma studied me suspiciously for a few moments before answering. "Yes, he said it's one of the worst cases of amnesia he's ever dealt with. Well, here's Dawn's number. You will have to memorize it: 555-512-5577. That's all I know, and we never had this talk." She turned her chair toward the front door. "Officer, we are done in here!"

I could tell by her face that she hadn't liked my response to the news. I was disappointed in my reaction as well.

As I walked back to my cell, I couldn't believe what I had just heard. I was relieved I hadn't killed

Dawn. I instantly felt better. I loved her, and I wanted her to be here with me forever. We had been born into this world together, and we should leave together. For the first time since being arrested, I felt good.

Before I got to my cell, I caught Matt's eye and he gave me the "watch your back" look. I could feel drama coming, but this time I was prepared.

The following day at breakfast, Mr. Lewis stood behind me in the breakfast line. I didn't want him anywhere near me because I had enough problems. I also despised pedophiles. I hadn't even liked him as a child, and I wanted him to know nothing had changed.

"My, how you've grown," he whispered from behind me. "Do you remember me, Damien?"

"Yeah, I remember you. Too bad I'm not a kid anymore, huh? Guess I'm not your type."

"Damien, I need your help in here. They are planning to kill me. I know I'm not perfect, but I didn't physically hurt those kids. Will you help me?"

"Hell no! If you were fucking with kids, you deserve whatever you get."

Mr. Lewis leaned close. "Well, I guess I'll have to tell everyone who you are. I'll have to let everyone know that you're sweet."

"Ain't nothing sweet about me. You've really lost

your mind, old man."

"Yes, you are. I always knew you were. That's why I loved having you in detention. A gay man can always tell. You hid it well, but not well enough to fool me."

"You trippin. I'm not helping you, and I hope they shove a broomstick up your ass."

"Well, after I tell everyone you are gay, maybe they will shove a broomstick up *both* our asses." He chuckled as he walked away.

I grabbed my tray and sat down, my mind racing at the thought of being exposed. I had completely lost my appetite, and I didn't know what to do about handling Mr. Lewis. The nerve of that fucking pedophile to try to blackmail me. I would rather die than help that sick pervert.

Matt abruptly interrupted my thoughts. "Hey, don't say I told you, but they are planning on stabbing you up in the shower tonight. I don't know if it's true but just be careful."

"Thanks for the heads up. I guess my balls will be dirty for a few days." Matt didn't laugh this time. I honestly didn't find it funny, either. I wasn't afraid to die, but I didn't want to die without seeing Mama again. I also wanted to make things right with Dawn and see if she really did have amnesia. My phone time was in the morning, so I planned on calling her then. I had memorized her number as soon as Emma gave it to me.

In the meantime, I could at least enjoy time away from my cell until Big Mike and his crew decided to kill me. After breakfast, I grabbed my book – I found it hidden beneath Crazy Joe's mattress – and headed out as the cell doors opened. "Where you think you going?" Crazy Joe quizzed. "You ain't learn your lesson the first time?"

"Guess not. I don't need to hear your speech today. I already know—when I leave, they leave."

"And what goes up comes down, too, motherfucka!" Crazy Joe called as I walked out. "Don't bring that bullshit to my house. I lived here first and don't have people leaving shit at my door for me to clean up!"

Surprisingly, there were no complications at rec. I even talked with a few people. I made eye contact with Mr. Lewis, who was peeking out of his cell. I decided to get him before he got me. I always get payback, and a person's biggest mistake is to tell me their plans. I stood up and stretched before walking toward my cell.

I cupped my hands, shouting for the whole prison to hear. "I just wanted to let everyone know, Lewis is a pedophile and he used to bother boys at my middle school. This sick pervert was my principal, and he always had a thing for kids. So what they are saying about him is true!"

"That's enough, Scott!" David yelled. "Get back to your cell!"

I felt contented as I lay in my cell. I had several reasons to be optimistic. First, I was safe from Mr. Lewis now—if he said anything bad about me, he would just look like he was trying to get revenge. Second, Dawn was alive. Third, the inmates were finally talking to me, and I was beginning to find my place in this new world. And fourth, I had survived another night in jail, which was never a guarantee.

Yes, things were starting to go my way. I rolled to my side and soon fell asleep. It wasn't long, though, before David's voice woke me up.

"Open up cell 101. Scott, get up! Come on, let's go!"

"Where am I going?" I asked, speaking loudly so that other prisoners would hear. I didn't trust David or any other correctional officer. I thought of all the movies I had seen where the guards bring you to a darkroom in a basement to beat you up or leave you to get gang-raped. I wasn't going without a fight.

"Get your stuff, Scott! You are going to pre-release. Your bail was posted."

"Nah, I don't believe you. No one posted my bail."

"Okay, dumbass. If you want to sit in prison when you don't have to, then I'll inform the judge you declined bail."

"If something happens to me, please tell everyone I went with David," I whispered to Crazy Joe. "You can have all my stuff!" I jumped down from the top bunk and walked out of the cell empty-handed.

Crazy Joe grunted. "I can have what stuff? This State shit? You don't have anything! Yeah, I'll see you soon. You'll be back! Your type always comes back." He fluffed his flat pillow and rolled over, unbothered.

4
FREEDOM

I grabbed the little brown bag containing my belongings and walked out of jail as fast as my feet could carry me. I walked six blocks before I reached a bus stop, where I waited for an hour for the bus.

I felt abandoned, sitting by myself in the cold. I didn't have a single person to call to pick me up from jail. I tried calling Dawn, but her phone just rang. At least I was free.

I got on the bus, but I had nowhere to go. I didn't have an address, a father's couch to crash on, a mother to call, or a sister to trust.

I wasn't one hundred percent convinced Dawn had amnesia. It just didn't sit right with me. Actually, things with Dawn hadn't sat right with me for a while now. I had started noticing how happy I was when I wasn't around her. But Dawn had never done anything to me; she was as close to perfect as a person can get. I couldn't figure out why I did mean things when she was around. I had wanted Craig to get something on her, something that could explain the weird things that happened in her presence. Instead, he had fallen in love with her and gotten her pregnant.

The bus stank, just like my life. I wasn't sure why I even kept waking up. For what? I looked out the dusty bus window and watched the people walking up and down the street. Some carried market bags, some looked like thugs, and some were regular-looking working people. The bus stopped at every corner, which annoyed me, but I wasn't in a rush. I didn't even know where I was going. I only had the lousy $300 I'd gotten from Dawn's house, and that wouldn't pay for many nights in a hotel. I wondered if my car was still parked at Dawn's. I looked in the brown bag which held my belongings and found my car keys. I decided to take the bus to Dawn's, just to grab my car.

I continued to look out the window as I sank deep into my thoughts. It was as if the bus slowed down to half speed, and suddenly there she was: Mama, standing in the middle of the crowd. I spotted her in the crowd.

I rang the bus bell continuously to get off at the next stop, my heart thumping with excitement. I couldn't believe it. I just wanted to hug Mama, smell her, and tell her I loved her. I missed her smell. She had a very peculiar smell.

I got off the bus and immediately ran back toward the previous stop, as fast as my legs could move. I didn't want to lose her again. I dodged through the outside crowd and even bumped a few people. Finally, I saw the back of her head. I instantly felt like everything was going to be alright. Mama would make it all better.

I got closer and closer, but Mama walked faster. I wondered whether she had seen me. Did she want to be lost? Did she not want a relationship with any of us anymore? She *had* left us with Sheryl. Maybe she didn't want to be found.

"Mama, Mama!" I screamed through the crowd, but she never turned around. I pushed through the last few people and tapped her arm. She turned around. It wasn't Mama—just some woman who was built like Mama and wore her hair the same way Mama did.

"Get your dirty hands off me!" she screamed, pulling away. "Have you lost your damn mind?"

"I'm sorry. I'm so sorry. I thought you were my mother."

"You don't know what your own mother looks

like? Grabbing on me like that! I don't even know you!"

"Apparently, I don't know what my mother looks like anymore," I muttered as I walked away. The woman went on complaining to anyone who would listen.

A heavy weight seemed to settle on my shoulders. Papa always said that a man should never cry or hang his head low, that it was a weakness for him to show his emotions. No matter how much I tried to shrug the incident off, though, I couldn't shake that terrible heaviness.

There was one person who could comfort me when I felt this way, and it was time I made the call. Luckily for me, my phone had been shut off when I got arrested, preserving the battery. It only had 10% when I powered it on, but it was enough for a phone call.

"Hello!" Craig answered rudely, already in a bad mood. "Who is this?"

"Hello, Craig. Who bit you in the ass?"

"Damien?"

"What other man do you have calling your phone? Or did you move on to someone else already?"

"Oh my God, Damien. Are you okay? I thought you were in jail. I'm so sorry about..." He trailed off.

"Yeah, someone bailed me out. I thought it was you, but by the tone of your voice, I guess it wasn't."

I frowned, not sure what to make of this. "Anyway, what are you sorry about?"

"Have you seen Dawn yet?"

"Is that Damien?" I heard a female voice whisper.

"No, I haven't seen Dawn yet," I replied. "Why? You know I'm not her favorite person after she caught us having sex."

I pressed the phone to my ear as I crossed the street. "Who was that asking about me?"

"That was nobody—one of my colleagues I talk to all the time about you." He hesitated. "I have some bad news."

"I can't take any more bad news. I thought this lady was Mama, and it wasn't, and it got me all fucked up. Not to mention, I just got out of jail a few hours ago. I'm dreading going to Dawn's apartment to pick up my car. I would hate to run into her in the garage or something."

"No! Don't go to Dawn's place!"

Craig's urgent tone surprised me. "Why not? I need my car—it's the only home I have until I figure some things out. I know she's pissed with me, but I'm not scared of Dawn."

"Tell him he can stay here," the female voice whispered.

"I don't think that's a good idea," Craig whispered back.

"Tell her thanks, but no thanks," I said. "I don't need to be a burden to anyone. Besides, I need some time to myself anyway."

"Let me pick you up, Damien. I'll take you to your car. Just stay with me tonight—I'll rent us a hotel. There's so much to talk about."

"You know what I really need? A hug."

"I know, Damien. I know. Where are you?"

"I'm near Tacoma Street, close to Gratiot. Hurry up, I just missed another bus."

"What the hell are you doing around there?"

"I saw a woman who looked like Mama, so I hopped off the bus. Look, it's a long story. Just come get me."

"On my way."

"My phone is dying, so I can't call you back, but I'll be waiting here."

Craig agreed, then said he'd see me soon. I heard the beep of a button, then a clatter. He must have tossed the phone aside, thinking he had ended the call when he had actually pressed the wrong button.

I stayed quiet, listening to his conversation with the woman who had been whispering to him before.

"I'm going with you! Just let me get my purse."

"Bella, you are not going. I can handle Damien. He needs me, and I'm still in love with him, so you just stay out of it!"

"No, I will not stay out of it. What if she is using him to get you there? Not to mention, it's dangerous around there. I'm going!"

"Bella, stop! Do you realize how crazy you sound right now? You know it's impossible for her to set me up. Did you already forget what happened to her? Stay out of this if you ever want us to fix our relationship. I mean it!"

That was the last thing I heard before my phone died.

I stood on the corner, wondering what I had just heard. Who was this Bella person, and why was she so concerned about Craig's safety? Maybe she was a good friend who had every right to feel suspicious, especially if Craig had told her about any of our nonsense. Shucks, I wouldn't trust us either. The only part that confused me was why Craig had said it was impossible for Dawn to set him up.

I decided to disregard the entire conversation. This Bella girl was just a worried friend, and I couldn't blame her.

It wasn't long before Craig was pulling up in his all-black Mercedes Benz, complete with red leather interior. I got in the car and looked around to see if we were alone before hugging him tightly. His arms felt comforting and warm. I felt safe to be myself for the first time in days.

Once we released each other, I studied his face. He looked terrible. His eyes were red and puffy, and the bags beneath them suggested he hadn't slept in days. I knew I wasn't looking too hot myself, but at least my black eye was going away. I saw a darkness in Craig's eyes that I had never seen before. Something horrible had happened to him. I wanted to know about it, but I didn't have the energy to sympathize. I was hurting enough on my own.

As Craig texted someone, I wondered why I had put him through so much. Maybe I had been afraid of love. Pushing him toward Dawn allowed me the freedom to avoid both my sexuality and the love he had for me. There was also the possibility I was afraid of abandonment, for which I could thank my absent mother. God, I missed her so much.

Craig's stress level seemed to be rising by the minute.

"What's going on?" I said as I buckled my seatbelt. "Why do you look so nervous?"

"I don't know where to start. Nothing makes sense—nothing!"

"Calm down. What's so bad that you can't just tell me? Start by saying the first thing that comes to mind."

"It's not that simple. There are other people involved, and I have to protect them too."

"Protect them from what?" I decided I was done dealing with his drama. "You know what, I don't have time for this stupid shit today. Just take me to Dawn's house so I can get my car."

"I can't."

"Why the hell not? Is this about that amnesia shit? I don't believe for one second her ass has amnesia, but I'm happy she's still alive."

Craig's head whipped toward me. "What are you talking about? Your sister's still alive?"

"Well, when you left the mountains that day, Dawn continued attacking me. She even cut my arm right here." I traced the scar Dawn had left me. "One thing led to another, and somehow she fell. I mean, I pushed her. I thought I had killed her, and I was beating myself up until I found out she was alive." I sighed with relief. "Damn, that felt good to finally tell someone that aloud."

"I had no idea all that happened. I hadn't seen Dawn since the mountains until…"

"Until what?" Craig lowered his head. When he kept silent, I went on talking.

"I'm just happy as hell my sister is still here, even if she is playing some crazy amnesia game. I will take her any way she comes at this point. A life without her wouldn't really be a life for me. I know we have a screwed-up family, but they are all I have. You know?"

"Yeah, I know. My family is all I have, too. I never told you much about my sister; it's a long story. She did something that's not sitting right with me, and it affects other people I care about. I've just been stressed."

Craig put on his blinker to make a right turn. He glanced out the rearview mirror, and his eyebrows rose.

"How bad could it have been that you can't deal with it? Craig? Why do you keep looking in the mirror?" I twisted my neck to look through the rear window. "Is someone following us?"

"No! Who would follow us? I don't want to talk about my sister anymore."

"Typical Craig. I tell you every disaster in my life, and you tell me nothing. You barely talk about your sister, as if she's a ghost or something. Never mind, don't tell me anything. I have enough of my own shit for both of us."

"It's not like that, Damien."

"This is not the way to Dawn's house. Where are we going?" I glanced in the side mirror and noticed the same silver Honda Accord was still behind us.

"I can't take you to Dawn's house right now. We are going to a hotel."

"I want my car! You are acting strange. Why are you avoiding Dawn's house so much? Are you scared of something? I know you haven't been still sleeping with her!"

"Damien, be for real. Wait a minute, let me just pull over."

Craig pulled the car over, and the silver Honda rode by. I felt relieved we weren't being followed.

"Why are we stopping?"

Craig took my hand. "I don't know how to tell you this, and I wish I didn't have to be the one, but Dawn is gone."

"Gone where?" I asked, pulling my hand away as my heart began to thump uncontrollably.

"She was shot. I'm so sorry, Damien. I'm so sorry."

He fell into my arms, crying. I sat there, stunned and unable to believe what he had just said.

"Someone shot Dawn? Is she dead? Are you sure? How do you know?" The words came out as quickly as my mouth could form them.

"I know you have questions, and I promise to answer them all. Right now, though, we have to go to the hotel. I'll take you to your car in the morning."

He sat up, knuckling away his tears with one hand and rubbing my shoulder with the other. "How do you feel? I know you and Dawn were really close, even when you were fighting."

"I honestly don't know how I feel. The last time I thought Dawn was dead in the mountains, she wasn't. I grieved really hard, cried every time I thought about her, and felt lost knowing she was no longer here. Almost like I lost a piece of me. The prison counselor just told me she was alive. This time, I will have to see her for myself. I feel like if she was dead, I would feel it, and I didn't feel it last time, and I don't feel it now." I paused. "If she's dead, where's her body?"

Craig put his seatbelt back on and merged into traffic. "I'm assuming the morgue. I'm not sure, though—I've been a wreck since it happened."

"I can't grieve again for nothing. Grief and guilt are not good for me right now. I have to see Dawn with my own eyes, so we can go in the morning."

I lay my head back as Craig drove, finally relaxing. I kept telling myself Dawn was okay. Then I thought of Mama, and my stomach ached. I had to find her while I was out on bail.

I had no intentions of returning to jail. If they wanted me, they would have to find me—no way in hell would I voluntarily turn my life over to the government to tell me when to eat and shit for life. I didn't even have a lawyer, and without one beating my charges would be impossible, so I just granted myself freedom. Screw the courts.

My gut kept telling me something was wrong. But I was with Craig, and he loved me. I decided to ignore the feeling. What could possibly go wrong? That would later prove to be my biggest mistake.

5

I OWN YOU

Craig and I finally arrived at the hotel. We parked the car on the street instead of the garage. I wondered why we didn't use the garage. Craig always spent money freely. He had it. Nothing but the best. It was one of the things I loved about him: he didn't settle for anything.

As I walked into the hotel, I was blown away by the building's elegance. There were enormous sparkling chandeliers, shiny marble floors with creme and gold decor. The place was absolutely fabulous. While Craig cockily approached the receptionist, I stayed behind and admired the beautiful hotel. A few people sat around a waterfall in the middle of the lobby. A man with a long beard sipped a steaming cup of tea. Two guys in business suits drank together and chatted. Two white women laughed as they went over their dinner plans, apparently waiting for their car to pick them up.

Then I noticed a single black woman sitting in front of the fountain reading a newspaper. She was absolutely stunning. Her legs were sexily crossed. Her fancy stilettos appeared brand new; I studied the bottom of her shoe, which showed no wear. She sat there in all black, her presence demanding attention. Her figure was impressive: her flat stomach, the way she sat in the eloquent velour chair.

She removed the newspaper from in front of her face, and we made eye contact for a split moment before she went back to reading.

I fell into deep thought, wondering why a woman of her class would be sitting there alone just reading junk in a newspaper in the evening. She was out of place, but so was I. I wanted to see her face again. She was seductive and extremely attractive. I wasn't into women, so I didn't know where this sudden infatuation was coming from. Every now and then, I run into a person who demands the room, and like any other human, I obey.

Craig walked up to me after leaving the receptionist's desk. He looked frustrated.

"Come on, let's go!" he demanded.

"Why? I'm so tired, Craig. Why can't we stay here? Are they all booked?"

"No. I left my wallet. I don't have any cash, cards, or anything on me. I rushed out to come and get you."

"Well, let's go. Where to now?" I glanced back to see the mysterious woman one last time. She was already gone. I briefly searched the room for her, but she had disappeared.

"We have to go up to the cabin," Craig said as we climbed into the car. "That's where my wallet is. We can't do anything without it."

"Your family cabin? We could just sleep in the car like we used to when we were sneaking around." I laughed at the memory as I buckled my seatbelt.

"Those were the fun days. Remember that time I told you to drink the bottle of water, and it was vodka? You choked and spat up all over the car." Craig laughed.

"That was not funny! You know I hate to drink."

"I miss those times with you, Damien. You were my balance, and I could always be myself around you. I wish we never involved Dawn in our life, I mean as your sister maybe, but not as a means to get information."

"I regret it too, Craig, more than you'll ever know. The worst part of all is, she never told you anything," I snickered.

"Right. Dawn is serious business. It took two years just for her to tell me her last name. That girl is tuff—*was* tuff, I mean."

"Is she really dead? Actually, don't answer that. I'll assume she's okay until I see otherwise. How long is this ride to the cabin?"

"You've been there before. The ski trip, remember? I didn't tell you that was my family cabin because it's a family rule to never bring outsiders to the cabin."

"Oh, no wonder you knew how to get to everything so easily. Of course I remember—we had sex in the snow, and I threw my twin sister off a mountain. How could I forget?"

"You mean we made love in the snow? Well, that all ended when Dawn came and almost killed our asses. I thought you were dead for sure." He laughed awkwardly.

"Did you see the look in her eyes? If she'd had a gun on her, we wouldn't be in this car right now, I'll tell you that."

"Okay, enough Dawn talk. When I get to the cabin, I'll run in to get my wallet, and then we're leaving right away. I don't know who in the family may be planning to stay there. You never know with my family. The last thing I need is my father to see me with a man in the middle of the night."

"I disagree, but I understand. I'll stay in the car."

We started our two-hour drive up to the cabin. The entire ride, we talked about old times. We laughed, kissed, and reminisced. Craig reminded me of why I loved him so much. It felt good to just leave the troubles of the world behind. It felt good to just be a regular couple taking a late-night ride. At least for the moment, that's what we were in my mind.

I often thought of Dawn, but I forced myself to think of something else. Craig really understood me, or maybe he was just so damaged himself that he overlooked my flaws. I think what Mr. Ralph did to him really screwed him up. Raping his own son and leaving him in a basement for months is torture. I'm happy that ugly sack of shit is dead. I just wish the police had found out who killed him. I also had hoped that Brianna would've shown up over the years, then I would be in the clear. She never showed up, though. I always said the day she showed up would be one of the happiest days of my life. It would prove my innocence.

Craig put on his blinker, and we turned off the main road. "While we're finally alone, I wanted to ask you something."

"Ask me anything," I responded, looking around the secluded area. It was dark, and all I could see was the shadows from the trees.

"Why did you kill my father?" he asked as he removed his seatbelt.

"What are we doing here? You're freaking me out."

"I know you are not scared. Not Mr. Damien. No, for real, why did you kill my father? I need to know."

"I didn't kill Mr. Ralph, Craig. Yes, I hated him, but I'm not capable of brutally murdering someone. That kind of person is an animal. But I did frame my father for his murder, which in turn made me look guilty."

"I had to ask. Ralph was a shitty father, but he was still my biological father. I had to know if the man I'm madly in love with actually murdered my father. Weird question, but I had to know. I'll help you get a lawyer. By the way, you can relax. I only stopped here to piss." He climbed out of the car.

"Oh, thank God. I thought you were stopping here to kill me or something." I laughed. "Thanks for offering to pay for a lawyer, but I'm never going back to jail, and I'm skipping out on bail. Instead of paying a lawyer, you can help me with some escape money. I need to get far away from these Detroit streets."

"I don't know about all of that, Damien. Running from the law? That's not a good life." Craig took care of his business, zipped his pants, and got back in the car.

"Going to jail is not a good life either."

We continued our drive and arrived at the cabin at 12:35 am. I was exhausted. I hadn't even been out of jail for twenty-four hours. All I wanted was a shower and a bed that didn't have a cellmate underneath it.

I stayed in the car as Craig had asked me to. I cracked the car window to feel the brisk night air; it felt like freedom. Craig had taken the keys with him so he could get into the cabin. I saw the living room light come on, and I hoped he would hurry up. The cabin made me think of Dawn. The last time I had seen Dawn was in this area when I had left her for dead. I wasn't too fond of this cabin.

"Damien, come in." Craig waved his hands, gesturing to me to come inside.

"Are you sure?" I whispered.

"Yeah! Come on, it's cold out there."

"Okay, give me a minute, I'll be in. Just give me five minutes."

Craig nodded and shut the screen door.

I hesitated before stepping foot out of the car. The snow on the ground immediately reminded me of where I was.

There's something inside all of us that tells us when something isn't right. Some call it guts; some call it intuition or instinct. Whatever it is, I felt it. I started questioning everything. Like maybe Dawn was alive, and she was waiting in that cabin to blow my brains out. Maybe she had bailed me out and used Craig to get me there.

My cell phone was dead, Craig had the car keys, and I was in the middle of nowhere at his family cabin. I hadn't been afraid the entire ride, but I had thought he was only getting his wallet. We were never supposed to stay. Now that the plans had changed, I felt uneasy.

I disregarded my intuition, though. I knew Craig loved me and would never set me up. I was being paranoid. I decided to let go and trust that I could have a typical night with my lover for once.

"Damien!" Craig yelled through the door. "What's wrong? Come on. It's getting cold in here from the door being open."

"I thought we weren't going to stay here!" I called back. "Why don't we just get the wallet and leave?"

When Craig didn't reply, I walked into the cabin. I removed my snow-filled shoes and walked toward the fireplace.

"It's late, and no one is here," Craig said. "We can just leave early in the morning because I'm tired of driving. Here, put on these dry socks." Craig handed me a pair of warm socks and joined me by the fireplace.

"This place just freaks me out a little. Maybe because…" I paused.

"Look, for tonight, let's just be together. No more talk about Dawn, bad memories, throwing people off mountains. Let's just be." He placed his hand on my knee. "My family spent a lot of time here, making pancakes, singing songs, and having snowball fights. This is a house of love. Don't overthink it, Damien."

"You are so right. I'm tripping, babe. Let me give you one of those massages you love." I began to massage Craig's muscular shoulders.

We talked for hours until we both drifted off to sleep.

"The nerve of you, thinking I would leave you alone," Mr. Ralph said, a large box in his hands. "You actually thought you could have a normal life after hurting us all? What a sick little freak you are!"

"I didn't hurt anyone. Why are you back again? Don't come closer. What's in the box?"

"Why am I back? The question should be, why are you back? Why are you back, Damien? Huh? Answer me! Why are you back?"

"I don't know. Please leave. Go away! Stay back!"

"No! I will never go away. Here, I have a little gift for you." Mr. Ralph handed me a box.

"I don't want it!" I screamed. "Just go, please go, please go!"

"Take it, boy!" he yelled, blood pouring from his

ears.

"Stop!" I yelled as I took the square box and forcefully opened it. I jumped back and screamed as I saw Mama's head in the box. I threw the box to the ground.

"Do you like your gift?" Mr. Ralph asked.

I jumped up from my sleep. My heart was thumping like a strong gorilla, and my forehead was sweating. My hands shook as I glanced around the cabin. I touched Craig to remind myself I was awake, to remind myself I was alive, but most importantly, that it had just been a nightmare. I gained my composure and started rubbing his hair.

I slowly rubbed his defined back. Craig turned over onto his back with his eyes still closed, and I began foreplay. I indulged his manhood in my warm mouth which instantly woke him up. He participated with moans and gentle pressure on my head as he pumped my mouth up and down. I continued to please him until he lifted my head up and motioned me to get on top.

Soon as I entered Craig's warm ass, I felt a cold metal sensation hit my head. It was so painful. I fell on my side as I was still partially inside Craig. I heard him screaming. Suddenly everything became a blur. I wasn't sure of anything, except that I had been attacked. Someone had knocked me out with something. Everything went black. I didn't know how long I was out, but when I opened my eyes a stunning woman appeared in front of me with a vicious look in her eyes. *Pure beauty* was my first thought as I felt the back of my head that quickly leaked blood.

"Get your bitch ass up!" I heard a woman scream as I moved my head in a circular motion. There was blood draining in my eyes, and I couldn't move. I heard a tea kettle loudly whistling.

"What's going on?" I asked in a low tone, still dazed from the blow I had taken to the head. Then I realized I was still naked, and my feet were tied to a chair. Craig appeared to be lying dead next to me, his legs and hands were tied. I panicked.

"Shut the fuck up! I'll tell you what's going on. Rule number one, don't talk unless I give you permission. Do you understand?" The woman's voice was familiar, but I couldn't quite place it.

"Yes. Is he dead?" I reached over to touch Craig, tears in my eyes.

"That wasn't me giving you permission," the woman said as she smacked my jaw with her gun. I screamed in pain.

"Oh yeah! Scream, daddy! That's how I like it. Maybe I should hit you again so you can scream louder. That's turning me on, more than that little dick of yours ever could."

"Can you please just get him some help?" I mumbled, afraid to speak.

"He's fine. I just gave him a few sleeping pills so I can talk to you. He's my brother. I would never hurt him, but you, on the other hand—you are not so lucky."

She threw a blanket over Craig's naked body. Then she grabbed a chair and sat in front of me. I recognized her, but I didn't know from where.

"Your brother? Oh, I'm sorry! May I speak?"

"Too late!" She smacked the other side of my jaw with the gun, harder than before. I felt one of my back teeth fall out. I spat the bloody tooth on the floor to avoid swallowing it. She moved closer, and I jerked back in fear.

"Ha ha! This is more funner than I thought. Did you lose a tooth, Danny Boy? I know how much you love your teeth." She roughly grabbed my jawline and squeezed my lips together. "Don't you recognize me? Go ahead, I'll give you permission to speak."

"I'm sorry, I'm not sure where I know you from," I stuttered.

"Oh, that's disappointing. You should know me very well. Let's play a game. I'll let you ask me three questions, and I will answer them honestly. Then I get to ask you three questions, and if I feel you are lying, I'll either shoot you or cut you with this knife." She picked up a sharp knife and pointed it at me.

"You want to play a game?"

"Don't worry, I won't kill you. Not for a few days anyway. I've waited far too long for this day. Now start your questions!"

I tried to play along and buy myself time until I could figure out how to escape. "How are you Craig's sister? What do you want with me? And why did you call me Danny Boy?"

"I'm Craig's sister because our parents adopted me after they found me in a burning house. I want to torture you. And for your last question, Danny Boy was the nickname your disturbed twin gave you." She frowned in disgust.

"My twin? Craig's sister?" I mumbled to myself in a confused tone.

"Yay! Now my turn to ask three questions! Do you know who I am now? Do you have powers too? Why did you do that to me?"

"I'm sorry," I pleaded as I realized who she was.

Craig stirred. "Do what to you, Bella? What the hell is going on? Release me!" He shook his head, trying to shrug off the effects of the pills.

"Damien is just about to answer my questions. Shut up, Craig, and listen to who your boyfriend really is. Speak now, Damien, before I shoot the first answer out of you."

"Yes, I think I know who you are now," I quietly answered. I was so confused, and I couldn't believe Brianna was right in front of me. My mind was racing, and I could tell she was getting impatient, so I answered the following question quickly. "I don't know what you mean by powers, but no, I don't have any. For your last question, I'm so sorry I did that to you, Brianna. I'm so so sorry."

"Did what to me, bitch? Say it out loud, you fucking coward! Say what you did!" Brianna sliced my right thigh, barely missing my penis.

"Calm down, Bella!" Craig said. "Put that damn knife away. What is going on with you? First Dawn, now this!"

"Tell him, Damien. Tell him! Tell him what you did!"

"I–I–I robbed you of your innocence," I stuttered, my head lowered as I looked at my thigh that was leaking blood. "I took your virginity to get back at my sister. I was young and stupid, and I just wanted Dawn to myself."

"Fuck all that 'robbed me of my innocence' bullshit. You raped me. Then your psycho-twin sister tried to kill me and set me on fire." She sliced my other thigh. I screamed again.

"Wait, you raped my sister?" Craig asked, tears in his eyes.

"No, Craig! I had rough sex with her, and the entire encounter was wrong, but I didn't rape her."

"You are a pathetic little liar!" Brianna yelled as she grabbed my penis hard and twisted it around. "You like to take this little dick and jam it into innocent little girls' vaginas, huh?" Her voice fell to a whisper. "Do you like to stick this scribbled-up dick in my brother's sweet ass, too?"

"No. I mean yes. I mean no, not little girls." I felt discombobulated. My penis was in the palms of her hands. For the first time ever, my dick had landed in the wrong hands.

"Ugh. You are so weak. All these little nappy hairs are making me sick. I think I'll just burn them off." Brianna frowned as she grabbed a grill lighter and set my pubic hair on fire. I screamed in excruciating pain. The smell of the burning hair made me sick to my stomach.

"Please, please, Brianna, please," I begged. "Don't burn me alive, please."

"Bella, that's enough!" Craig shouted. "Untie me now!"

"But that's what y'all did to me. Y'all set me on fire! Like I was nothing. Like I didn't have a life and parents that loved me. Did you or Dawn ever stop to think I was a person? I was a person that was loved. I was a normal sweet girl, with a loving home. You took that from me. You both did!"

"Bella, I understand you are upset," Craig began. "I promise you, I do. Please let me go so I can stop this before more damage is done."

"Oh, shut up. I'm not going to burn his shitty ass alive. At least, not right now."

Brianna walked to the kitchen as the flames on my pubic hair began to turn into dust. She grabbed the tea kettle that had been whistling since I regained consciousness. She threw it on the remaining flames, scalding me. There was a mist of smoke from the boiling water and the leftover flames.

"You fucking crazy bitch! No, I'm sorry, I didn't mean that. Brianna, I'm sorry. Please stop, please. I can't take anymore. My dick is burning. Craig, it's burning! Please help me. Please. It's blistering. Stop! I need an ambulance. Please, please." I didn't think I could endure any more pain.

"Oh, I know what fire burning on skin feels like. Look at my neck! Look at it, motherfucker!"

"Brianna, I'm not the one who set you on fire. I didn't even know Dawn did that to you. I had no idea, I swear. Dawn was always so innocent. Now I know why her hair smelled like smoke that day. Ask your brother! Ask him. I made him start dating Dawn to get some information about her. I started suspecting she was crazy, even crazier than me. I just got blamed for everything. It wasn't me. I swear."

"Craig, you know I love you and would never hurt you," Brianna said, waving the gun around as she talked, "but I want you to tell me the truth. How did you start dating Dawn?"

"He's telling the truth. I met Damien first; we actually met as little kids. He was the first boy I ever liked."

"I told you!" I screamed.

"Shut up!" Craig continue," Brianna demanded.

"I ran into him when we were older—I knew who he was, but he didn't remember me. We dated in secrecy for a while before he suggested I date Dawn to see if she was evil, and in return, we could always see each other in the open. He said if Dawn was who he thought she was, he would be free if she was exposed. That's all I know."

"See, I'm telling the truth!" I cried.

"Stop all of that crying!" Brianna demanded. "What made you start suspecting Dawn?" she asked me with the gun rested to her side.

"It was at my Aunt Sheryl's house. Sheryl wasn't a good person. I'll admit, I tortured her by leaving her pissy on the floor for weeks, but Dawn did something out of this world. She still doesn't know I know." A stream of tears ran down my face. I wanted to be tough, but having my penis scalded made it a little challenging.

"What did she do?"

"If I say it, it won't make sense."

"If I kill you right now, it will make sense. Talk!"

"Dawn muted my aunt; she stopped her from ever speaking again. She did the same thing to my Uncle Robby. I had no proof, but one day I decided to be nice to Sheryl; that's what we called her—just regular Sheryl, not 'aunt'. Sheryl wrote on a piece of paper that Dawn had pushed her down the steps and taken her voice. I told her to stop lying, but I actually believed her. See, I love Dawn. She is the only person besides Craig and Mama who truly loved me."

Brianna cut me off before I could finish explaining. "Do you really think I give a fuck about who loves you? My life was stolen from me. All I want is to hug my mother—my real mother. I want to jump into my father's arms and hear him call me 'baby girl' just one more time." She knuckled a tear off her face.

"Bella, you don't have to be missing anymore," Craig said. "I'll help you find your parents."

"You don't understand, Craig. Dawn is demonic. She will torture my parents just to get to me, so I can't reconnect with them until I know she's dead."

"She *is* dead! You killed her, remember?" Craig raised his eyebrows.

"Is that why you wouldn't tell me what happened to her?" I said. "You were protecting your sister?"

"Did I give you permission to speak?" Brianna slapped my face, this time with her bare hands.

"Damien, don't talk to me right now," Craig said. "You have more secrets than I'm willing to deal with." He turned back to his sister. "Brianna, Dawn is dead. I checked her pulse myself. You shot her in the head. She's gone!"

"She's not gone! I had a nightmare last night. She is very much alive." Fear flashed in Brianna's eyes. "Did you have one too, Damien?"

"I did. But what do my nightmares have to do with anything?" I closed my eyes. It seemed to help with the pain.

"Dawn is more powerful than you know. She creates the nightmares we have. She admitted that to me right before I shot her. It's one of her ways of controlling people. When she thought I was dead, the nightmares stopped. Now that she knows I'm alive, they are back. Which told me she was alive. I also called someone to confirm it."

"Mama and Papa got them, too," I observed. "Everyone had nightmares except Dawn." Then I flinched, realizing I hadn't asked for permission to speak. For the first time, though, Brianna didn't hit me.

"Okay, Bella," Craig said, "we will figure out how to tame Dawn so you can be reunited with your family. You have to let Damien go, though."

"I will do no such thing. Damien will take me to Dawn, and I will kill her—this time for good."

Brianna walked over to me, tied my hands up with more thick rope. Next, she did the unthinkable, she cut open my shoulder, and placed a chip inside. She then sewed my skin up like it was a piece of fabric. I screamed through the entire process. Craig couldn't bear to watch.

Craig sounded queasy. "Bella, come on. Stop this!"

"Now I have a tracking device on you. If you try to run, I will know where you are, and I'll just call the police. You are a murderer out on bail, and I own you. One phone call and back to jail you go. If you try to take it out, it will blow up, and you will die.

"A device that will blow up? What is this some type of action movie?" I mumbled, calling her bluff.

"In case you forgot, Craig and I family are wealthy. With money, anything is possible. Either way, I own you. Now sit there and figure out how to get Dawn to me. I'll be back in a few days." She took the knife and cut the rope from Craig's hands and feet. "Craig, get dressed, and let's go!"

She untied Craig and they both left the room. Shortly after, I heard the front door shut, and then I listened to the cars pull out.

That fucking crazy bitch Brianna has lost her fucking

mind! I thought. *I played nice to save my life, but she messed up, leaving me alive. Scalding my penis, torturing me like I'm not who I am. I'm Damien, and clearly, she forgot that I'm the real fucking monster. Mr. Nice guy is gone. She had the nerve to tell me she owns me. She owns me? I'm going to show her who's the boss. I should've ripped her anus open when I took her in the fields. With her dry ass pussy. Who does she think she is? She left me in the dark with two cut wounds, burnt penis hair, two missing teeth, and a sewed-up arm, and she really thinks I'm going to be her little puppet. And that damn Dawn, that nut job was behind everything all along.*

Dawn actually fooled everyone into thinking she was an innocent child, when all along she was secretly torturing the whole damn family. I knew she was evil; I just had no way of proving it. Now that I know Craig and Brianna are related, he can no longer be trusted. Craig was always weak, but I didn't see this coming. So, Brianna must have been in the silver Honda that was following us. I'm still amazed at how beautiful she is. Her body and face are flawless. She literally looked like a supermodel. I guess that's what growing into your looks means.

I must get out of here before Brianna returns. She's capable of anything. Shit, she is almost as crazy as Dawn. I can't believe I actually wanted Brianna to be alive so I wouldn't be a suspect in her disappearance. She sure looked alive to me. I wonder if Dawn killed Mr. Ralph, too? She must've.

Ugh, my penis really hurts. Brianna wanted to keep calling my man-piece little. She repeatedly said, little dick this, little dick that. It was soft; what does she expect? She tried to break my ego and my self-esteem. I'm going to break her ass in half.

Brianna just don't know that she opened up something inside of me that I've been trying to keep quiet. I might not have mental powers, but I'm clearly more dangerous than Dawn. First, I'll help Brianna get to Dawn, because if she can get rid of her, I won't have to. Now that it's been confirmed that Dawn was doing everything, it's either me or her. I choose me. As for Brianna, I'll give her something way worse than rape, and I'll show her who owns who!

6
PAPA'S TURN

Papa had been to the hospital every day since Dawn was admitted. He also looked for Mama a lot, but to no avail. He didn't have a clue where she was, but he knew she didn't really want to be part of the family anymore.

Meanwhile, Papa had fallen in love with someone else. He met her the day after he was released. He didn't know how Dawn would feel about him seeing another woman, so he kept the relationship private. Damien knew Papa was a whore, but Dawn was always in denial.

Papa was in the best shape of his life, and he felt it. His caramel skin, muscular arms, and rough curly hair attracted a lot of attention from the ladies.

The day Papa met his beautiful new girlfriend was a day he would never forget. He only had about fifteen dollars to his name. Unfortunately, they don't give you anything to start a new life when they release you from jail: no clothes, money, housing, job, nothing. You are all on your own. Luckily Papa had twenty-eight dollars left in his prison account from working in the jail's kitchen.

Papa was popular in prison. He got in a few fights here and there but always won. His name carried considerable weight on the inside.

Papa went into a Dunkin Donuts, not knowing where he would sleep that night or get his next dollar from. He had too much pride to ask Dawn for help. He ordered a coffee and wished he had a real drink. He was done with liquor, but he still had the occasional urges. The cashier rang up the cup of coffee, and Papa fumbled around in his pockets for some change. He looked up with two balled-up dollars in his hand, and there she was, as if she had just fallen out of the sky: young, beautiful, strong, and in charge. He'd never forget what she said, and it still made him laugh when he remembered it.

"I'll buy that for you, gorgeous," the beautiful young woman said to Papa.

He couldn't believe she had called him gorgeous. She was the best-looking woman he had seen in years. She was on Mama's level but younger. They spent every day together from that moment forward. She was perfect. She never complained. She was good in bed. She didn't have any kids. For the first time ever, Papa was actually faithful. He was madly in love, and there was nothing more he wanted than to spend every moment with her.

He was grateful when she moved him into her luxury condo apartment, and he worked very hard to pay her back. She rarely accepted Papa's money, though. He just couldn't understand how he had gotten so lucky.

"Jerome!" Brianna said. "Baby, did you hear me calling you?"

"I'm sorry, my love. I was just daydreaming about Dawn again. For real, Bella, this shit got my head fucked up. How was your work trip? You've been gone for an entire week. We have some making up to do." He grabbed Brianna's waist and pulled her closer to him.

"Why are you so crazy? I've missed you too. I'm sorry I couldn't use a phone on the work retreat. Catch me up on Dawn. Is she okay?"

"No! Some motherfucker shot her. They shot my baby, and she is in the ICU."

"Someone shot her? I thought she slipped off a mountain? Jerome, I'm so sorry I wasn't there to support you. Do they have any suspects?"

"No, Bella. And she hasn't fully woken up yet. I know she will come back to me. I'm not giving up on her—she's all I have besides you."

"Well, you do have your son, too," Brianna said, rubbing Papa's arm.

"Bella, don't start that shit. I told you, Damien is dead to me!"

"Don't 'Bella' me. I just think you need to forgive him. Family is family, you know. Speaking of family, when do you think I can meet them? It's been months."

"Damien? Never! Dawn will take some time. She can be a bit jealous. I think at times she was even envious of her mother. I know that sounds crazy, but she's a true daddy's girl."

"Well, at least let me go to the hospital with you to bring her some flowers and love. You said she's unconscious, right? She won't even know I was there."

"But what if she happens to wake up while you are there? How will I explain this pretty hot young lady that's her age in her daddy's arms?"

"Jerome, please. What are the chances of her waking up at that very moment? If she does, I'll just play it off."

"No, Bella. I don't want you to meet my princess

like that. She's all hooked up to machines, and they cut off all her hair. It's bad, and I'm going to figure out who did this. When I do, I'll blow their fucking head clean off their shoulders!"

"You should let the police handle it. I couldn't deal with you going back to jail and being taken away from me. That would destroy me."

"I would never leave you, baby, and I won't get caught. That's enough about that. I'm your daddy right now. Come sit on Daddy's lap. I've missed you so much, girl." Papa grabbed Brianna, and they laughed as they fell into bed together.

Papa wasted no time removing Brianna's panties with his mouth as he caressed her breast with his hands. He began licking her clitoris softly and gently as Brianna moaned. She grabbed his curly head and shoved it roughly into her vagina, and Papa sucked sloppy and rough as she liked it. Brianna released all over Papa's face, and he continued to lick. She forcefully pushed his head away, and he laughed.

He loved when she couldn't take it anymore. He laid on his back and waited for her to get on top. His favorite position was for a woman to ride. Brianna slowly got on top and swayed her hips from side to side, then she moved up and down on Papa's long hard stiff, fully erected penis. He moaned as he grabbed her waist to make her move faster. He pumped harder and rougher. She slowed him down to remind him she was in control. He obliged and sucked her breast intensely.

"Say my name," she whispered.

"Hmmm, don't stop, baby," Papa responded.

"Say my name," she moaned.

"Bella, Bella, oh yes, Bella," Papa moaned as he released his semen in Brianna's perfectly lubricated vagina.

"Hmmmmm, yes," she moaned and pumped harder. She released her second orgasm and fell on the bed in exhaustion.

"I love you so much, Bella," Papa said, putting his arms around Brianna.

"I love you, too," she replied, still breathing heavily. "Do me being only twenty-three bother you sometimes?"

"No. It's not like you are eighteen or something. You are very mature. I'm the immature one, so it's like we are the same age." He laughed.

"I mean, I am your kids' age. It doesn't bother me because I love older men, but I thought maybe that's why you won't let me meet Dawn. Like maybe you are ashamed of me or something."

"Are you crazy? Hell no, I'm not ashamed of the most beautiful woman in Detroit. I'm just a little concerned about how Dawn will take it because of her mother."

"Yeah, I keep forgetting that you are still married," Brianna said sarcastically as she covered her naked body with a sheet.

"Don't start that again, Bella. I will start working on the divorce as soon as I find her. I promise."

"Isn't that what all men say?" She laughed.

"Where is all this coming from? We talked about my situation, and you said you understood. It's not like my wife is in the picture; we don't even know where she is."

"I don't know. I'm just committing so much of myself to you, and you keep everything from me." Brianna's voice was soft, regretful.

Papa sighed in frustration. "Girl, you always break me down, especially after you throw that thing on me. You can come to the hospital with me tomorrow. Will that make you happy?"

"That will make me very happy! But I need it to be today. I have a big meeting tomorrow that I can't miss."

"Okay, whatever you want." He stared into Brianna's eyes. "Let me ask you a question. Are you ashamed of *my* age? I haven't met any of *your* family, either."

"My parents would not be okay with your age, especially not my father. Baby, I will have to ease this on them. You can't meet my brother either because he will tell my parents—trust me, he can't hold water. Just give me a little more time, and I'll tell them."

"Oh, so you can take your time introducing me to your family, but with me it's unacceptable?"

"It's different, Jerome. I don't have kids and a wife."

"Yeah, ard. I think I need round two before we get ready for the hospital." Papa smirked.

"No! I need to shower. I want to have time to stop and get Dawn some flowers. I'm so excited! This means so much to me. Thanks, baby, for opening up today. I'll have something for you tonight." She jumped off the bed, grabbed her robe, and went to the bathroom to shower.

Papa was older, but he wasn't naive. He checked Brianna's phone while she was in the shower. Her passcode was 911; he had seen her put it in many times. She had no calls in her recent activity except for Papa's calls on the day she left for her work retreat. So it appeared her phone had been off for a week, as she had said. Papa didn't know how to maneuver through cell phones very well, but he was able to open up one text message from Craig:

"Bella. I'm so disappointed in you. I can't stop thinking about what happened. It was a side of you I've never seen, and

I can't stop replaying it. Call me back, and oh yeah, if you act like them, you are no different than them! Call me back."

Papa heard the shower cut off. He fumbled to close the text message. He heard Brianna step out of the shower. He finally got the phone back to the home screen and hit the lock button. He quickly placed the phone back where it was, just as she stepped into the room. Brianna gave him a weird look, and he smiled. He couldn't believe what he had read. He didn't understand it. What was her brother talking about? It didn't sound like the Bella he knew. All kinds of thoughts popped into his mind. He wished he hadn't read it.

Papa knew he couldn't ask her about it, or it would instantly break their trust. How could he explain what he had been doing with her phone in the first place? Papa thought maybe Bella had stolen something. He couldn't imagine her doing anything harmful. Just as he decided to forget about it and be grateful she hadn't been cheating for an entire week, her phone rang. Papa glanced over to see who was calling. It was her brother Craig, and she hit the decline button.

"Why didn't you answer the phone?" Papa asked.

"It's just Craig being annoying, plus he's a little upset with me," she confessed.

"Why?" Papa eagerly asked.

"I don't want to talk about it!"

"I do. I want to know more about you, Bella." He was fishing for any information he could get. "It's funny that your brother's name is Craig. My daughter dates a guy named Craig, too. What does your brother look like?"

"He's tall. But how he looks doesn't matter." Brianna chuckled.

Papa was searching the closet for something to wear. "What's so funny? What if Dawn is dating your brother Craig? That would be some freaky shit, huh?"

"Freaky shit is right, especially since my brother is gay. Unless Dawn is a man with a hard stiff dick, I seriously doubt my Craig is the Craig you are thinking of." She laughed.

"Ohhhh. I never knew your brother was gay. Yeah, it's definitely not the same Craig. Dawn and I both despise that gay shit."

"Excuse me? Why should you be bothered by the way someone else lives? That bullshit you said just pissed me off. Everyone should be allowed to be who they are. Who are you to judge?"

"Calm down. I understand it's a touchy subject. I just believe men should be with women, which is how we keep human creation. I'm allowed my opinion, right?" He grabbed a towel.

Brianna stared into the vanity while applying mascara to her almond-shaped eyes. "Your opinion is stupid. If every person worried about themselves, the world would be a better place."

"Look, let's not fight," Papa said, standing in the bathroom doorway, his muscles sweaty and a towel wrapped around his waist. "We just made love. I'll be open to Craig; it still doesn't mean I accept or agree with his lifestyle, but I will respect him as your brother. Now, why was he upset with you in the first place?"

"It was nothing really. I got into a fight with my parents, and I disrespected them for the first time ever. I even cursed at my mom." Brianna rubbed lotion up and down her long, fit legs. "Craig was appalled. He said I should never act like them; I should've kept my cool and been respectful. My parents can be so obnoxious, though."

"Oh damn, that's crazy. I'm sure your parents will forgive you, though." Papa was relieved to know his precious Bella hadn't done something he couldn't live with. He kissed her on the cheek and walked inside the double-glass shower.

"That'll teach you next time not to snoop through my damn phone," Brianna said under her breath with a smirk.

"Did you say something, baby?" Papa yelled from the bathroom.

94

"No! I was talking to myself!" Brianna yelled back as she continued getting dressed.

It wasn't long before they were on their way to the hospital. They stopped at a local flower shop, and Brianna picked up a bundle of daisies. Papa was impressed she'd happened to pick up Dawn's favorite flowers. He felt good about taking Bella to the hospital. He wanted nothing more than for Dawn to wake up. It pained him to see her there. To leave his baby girl in the cold hospital room was something that constantly bothered him.

They arrived at the hospital, and Brianna walked away from the check-in desk while Papa checked in. She said she had to use the bathroom. She met Papa back at the elevator. They rode up to the tenth floor and got off. Brianna was nervous. She hadn't planned on getting this close to Dawn so soon. She wished she had something to put in Dawn's IV to kill her, but all she had were some daisies.

They entered the room, and Dawn was still unresponsive. Papa immediately looked disappointed. Brianna grabbed his hand and squeezed it. Papa hugged her. He sat in a chair next to Dawn and kissed her cheek.

"I'm here, baby. You keep fighting in there. I'm waiting for you to come back to me."

Brianna just stood over her, staring without so much as blinking.

"Mr. Jerome, just the guy I was looking for," Dr. Smidget said as he entered. "How are you today? I see you have some support with you this time." He gave Brianna a gentle smile.

"Hey, doc. Yes, this is my friend Bella. Any updates on Dawn's progress?"

"Let's talk in the hallway. Nice to meet you, Bella."

Brianna shook the doctor's hand and watched Papa and Dr. Smidget leave the room. She moved closer to Dawn.

"Hey, you evil little bitch. I bet you didn't expect to hear my voice in your little sick mind. I know you are in there because you started the nightmares again. Don't worry, I won't let you live. Since shooting you didn't work, I'm going to chop your fucking head off and mail it to your precious Papa—who, by the way, I'm fucking. His dick is so good, too. I love sitting on your daddy's dick. Every time I fuck him, I make him say my name, and I think of you.

She leaned close and whispered in Dawn's ear. "I even thought of getting pregnant, but I would hate to have an evil child like you or Damien. Are you afraid? Can you hear me, bitch? I'm coming for you, and this time I won't fuck up."

Brianna heard the door opening and moved back.

"Look who's not acting shy anymore," Papa said.

"I just had to say a quick prayer for her. It's all I know how to do in a time like this. Jerome, this is a lot for you. It's a lot for me, and I don't even know her. Hopefully, this will all be over soon."

"Well, Dr. Smidget finally gave me some good news. He said Dawn had brain activity yesterday. So now she can wake up whenever her body feels up to it." He rubbed his forehead, unable to believe his fortune. "This is the best news I've had since this happened a week ago."

"That's great news!" Brianna said, pretending to be pleased. "Are you ready? Let's grab lunch. Maybe when you come back tomorrow, she'll be awake."

"Wouldn't that be something?" Papa asked with the biggest smile on his face. They left the room holding hands.

"Oh, crap," Brianna said, searching her pockets and purse. "I forgot my phone. Let me run back into the room and get it."

Papa sat beside the elevator. "Okay, babe. But hurry up—I'm starving."

Back in the hospital room, Brianna leaned close to Dawn again. "One more thing, you little rotten bitch: I have Damien. Craig is also on my side. You have no one. I'll turn your father against you, too! I wish I had enough time to smother you with this pillow, but you deserve much worse. I'll be waiting for you, Danny girl."

"That was fast," Papa said as Brianna returned. "Did you find it?"

"Find what?" Brianna asked, distracted and bothered.

"Your phone, crazy. Did you find it?"

"Oh, yes, I found it. Thanks. Are you ready?"

"Are you okay? You look off. Did something upset you?"

Brianna put a hand to the side of her head. "I'm fine, Jerome. I just got a little lightheaded. Probably need to eat."

They entered the elevator. They went one floor down, and two men entered the elevator.

"Jerome, long time no see," Detective Ross stated, holding his hand out for a handshake.

"Hey, Ross, man," Papa said as he shook Detective Ross's hand. "Hunny, this is the detective I told you about. He's the one that locked me up and came back to get me released. Crazy, right?"

"Hi. Well, I'm glad you got Jerome released. I don't know what my life would be without him. Nice to meet you," Brianna gave Papa's hand a tight, comforting squeeze.

"You look very familiar," the detective said. "What was your name again?"

"Bella," Brianna stated nonchalantly. "Well, that's our stop!" She rushed off the elevator. Detective

Ross put his foot in the doorway to stop the elevator from closing.

"I know your face very well," Detective Ross insisted. "It's a face I looked at many times, but from where?"

The elevator started beeping.

"I'm not sure, sir, nor am I from Detroit," Brianna answered as she and Papa began walking away. "You gentlemen have a nice day."

"Damn, you are such a badass!" Papa said in an embarrassingly-loud voice. "That's right! We don't talk to the motherfucking cops. I like how you said, *gentlemen*. That's how you handle them bitches! Girl, you are just full of surprises."

"You have no idea!" Brianna said.

7
DAMIEN'S TURN

I'd been blacking in and out for the last two days. I assumed it had been two days because I had seen the sun at least twice. I was dehydrated, and I was pretty sure my body thought it was dying. It's pretty messed up to leave someone alone in the dark.

I hallucinated a lot. I'd never spent that much time by myself. My thoughts became random and dangerous. I'd been self-sabotaging. The likelihood of someone finding me was slim to none. My emotions had changed from anger to pity. I wanted someone to help me. I wanted to cover up my exposed body. I'd been freezing and naked for days. At least my penis didn't hurt anymore. I didn't know if that was a good or bad thing. Losing feeling might have meant it didn't work anymore, or maybe my body was stressed because I hadn't had food or water. This was worse than how I had treated Sheryl. At least I had fed her. I mean, it was cat food and toilet water, but I didn't leave her to die.

I pissed myself twice, but luckily I hadn't had to make a bowel movement. I hadn't actually had any food since I was in jail—Craig and I had never made it to the hotel restaurant. I kept telling myself religious people fasted all the time, so I'd be fine. My mind was deteriorating by the minute.

Everything was getting stranger and stranger. I kept having an urge to hug Mama. I was starting to feel obsessed with her. I thought about her morning, noon, and night.

I heard a door slam. I felt a ball of emotions. I was happy that someone else was in the house; I hoped it was Craig and not Brianna. Just thinking of Brianna made me angry. I knew I would have to be calm and polite to get some food or something from her, but inside I was furious.

"Hey, pissy! Awww, you look disappointed. Were you hoping I was Craig?"

Brianna was wearing a yellow Armani suit that fit her perfectly. She had left the silk blouse partially unbuttoned, and for some strange reason, that grabbed my attention. She was a dime, and it was hard not to notice, even for a gay man. Her beauty and style were undeniable.

"Hi, Brianna. Honestly, I didn't care who it was—I'm just happy I wasn't left here to die."

"I'm sorry it took me so long to get back to you. I was busy fucking your father." She laughed as she got closer with a bottle of water. My throat did a dance for joy with the hope of possibly getting some water. She poured almost the entire bottle on the floor and laughed.

"Brianna, I need water. Please," I begged completely ignoring what she said about sleeping with Papa.

"You are turning into such a little bitch. Always whining and complaining. Where is the tough Damien, huh? The one that tortured cats and shit when we were young. The one who raped me. That's who I want to torture. This weak man who sits before me is a pussy, and I don't like it."

"Brianna, I need—" I began, but she smacked me with the gun before I could say more.

"Did I tell you to speak? Oh, you forgot the rules again. You definitely can't speak if you are going to be crying and shit. Here, take some water." She poured a squeeze of water down my throat. I choked and drank as much as I possibly could. I raised my hand to speak, and she gave me permission with a nod.

"So, when are you going to release me?" I asked.

"What's your aunt's name again?" Brianna asked, changing the topic.

"Sheryl. Why?"

"You don't ask me why. Here's the plan; I will release you today. It's too much of a burden to keep coming here to check on you. Dawn will be waking up soon. I need you to convince her to stay at your father's house when she gets out of the hospital. Tell her you are sorry for everything and you will never cross her again. I just need you to take her to your father's to heal. I'll take it from there."

"How do I know you won't kill me?"

"You don't. This is your only chance. Don't cross me, and I'll let you live. As far as everyone is concerned, I'm still missing. There's only one person that can ruin my life, and her name is Dawn. I'll kill her and leave your life forever."

"Why my father's house? He hates me, and he will never let me in."

"I'm working on that. You just do your part."

"So you will just let me go, and I'm supposed to go back to my life like everything is normal?"

"Hell no. I don't trust you. I will put you in the trunk of my car while I drive back to the city. Craig has a hotel room in his name; you can shower, eat, and get dressed. I have a phone for you that I will call you on. I don't want you bumping into your father at the hospital—that may ruin everything, so wait for my call. When I call, you answer! Don't forget you have a chip inside you. I will know your every move."

"And if I don't comply?"

"I'll just blow you up, Damien. No skin off my nose! I'll get to Dawn another way. If you think the chip is a bluff, I would strongly recommend you reconsider. My beautiful adoptive family has more money than you could ever count. That gives us access to things that the ordinary public doesn't even know about. One good thing that came out of this for Craig and me was wealth. Please don't underestimate it."

She threw me a cheesy outfit that must've been her dad's.

"I would turn around and get dressed, but you've seen every inch of me naked, so there's really no need," I said as I rushed to put my clothes on. Brianna never took the gun off me or even blinked.

"Okay, here's how this is gonna go. You walk up the steps first, open the door, and get directly in the trunk. Don't try anything stupid or you'll get a bullet in the back."

I rode for two hours in the trunk of the car. It was the same small Honda coupe I had seen following Craig and me when he allegedly forgot his wallet. I knew it wasn't Brianna's car because she was too wealthy to be riding in a Honda, so I assumed it was a rental.

The trunk was tight, dark, and closed in. After a while, I started hearing people talk, and I noticed the regular street chatter. I felt relieved. I knew I was back in the city. I knew Brianna wasn't dropping me off in a ditch. Brianna pulled the car into an alley tucked away from the main streets.

"Okay, Damien. This is when we start trusting each other. I can't drag you into a hotel tied up with a gun to your back. You will have to drive yourself to the hotel, and I'll sit in the passenger seat, still with the gun on you. You need to start calling me Bella. No slip-ups. Only Bella—Brianna is dead. Once we arrive at the hotel, you get out and go straight to the penthouse. Here's the key." She handed me the room key as I stretched my sore muscles.

I drove myself to the hotel and went to the room, as promised. It was the same hotel Craig and I had visited before. The room was gorgeous. I couldn't believe they had put me in such a nice hotel room. There was food already prepared on the table: sandwiches, fruit salads, chips, and drinks.

I dug straight in like a stray dog. I almost lost my appetite when I caught a whiff of how horrible I smelled. Since the morning I'd left the jail, I hadn't had a shower, and the urine smell was still stuck in my skin.

Right after I ate, I took a shower. It was the best shower ever. I was grateful for everything at that moment. I brushed my teeth about four times before I finally made my way to the bed. I honestly didn't even have the energy to try to escape. I also believed Brianna had put a real chip inside me. Dawn and I had ruined her life—of course she had invested in something to ensure she was safe. I also knew they had money, so I wasn't taking any chances of getting blown the fuck up. I really just wanted to lie on the plush mattress and go to sleep. Before I could do so, though, I noticed a flip phone resting on the dresser, a note taped to it.

Damien,

Here's the phone I promised. So far, I've kept my word. Now make sure you keep yours. I would hate to see the housekeepers clean up such a mess.

Answer this phone no matter what! Keep it charged. Do not leave the hotel. You can wander the lobby and go to the hotel's restaurant, but I repeat, do not leave the hotel. Anything you need, just charge it to the room. I'll talk to you soon.

I balled up the note and threw it on the floor. I thought of calling Craig to give him a piece of my mind, but what would that accomplish? He already thought I was a rapist.

I lay under the sheets and started jerking my sore penis. I didn't actually want to masturbate; I wanted to make sure I still had feelings down there. It was too sore to tell, so I just stopped.

Although I was tired, I had too many thoughts racing through my mind to fall asleep. I snatched the cellphone and the room key and left the room. I sat in a nice area in the hotel where they provided complimentary glasses of wine. An older white guy was playing the piano. My mind drifted off into a daydream.

Whenever I thought about what had happened to me, I grew furious. I couldn't just pretend Brianna hadn't tortured me and left me ass-naked with burnt pubic hair. I started wondering if I deserved what had happened to me.

My mind went back to the day I saw the yellow tape around Mr. Ralph's house. Earlier that day, Papa had slapped the living hell out of me, and that was actually the moment that had changed everything. That violent slap encouraged me to send him to prison for Mr. Ralph's murder.

I then started thinking about how Dawn and I

would ride our bikes when we were much younger. While riding our bikes, I chased a cat down with a stick one day, and Dawn just watched. She never said, "Damien, stop! Leave the poor cat alone." She let me chase the cat, torture the cat, and right when I went in for the kill, she said, "Stop! What's wrong with you?"

What was wrong with *her*? Why had she let me get that far before saying something? Who in their right mind would watch someone torture and beat a helpless animal?

Someone who enjoys it, that's who, I thought.

8
BELLA VS BRIANNA

Brianna was struggling to keep up with her new lifestyle. She had turned into a killer, sleeping with an older man for revenge and disappointing her brother. Secretly Brianna was falling for Jerome. He was handsome, with muscles and a pleasurable penis. He was a manly man, and he turned Brianna on.

But Papa knew Bella, not Brianna. He had been under arrest when Brianna went missing, and he had never really paid her any attention before that. Brianna knew he would never recognize the older her. All the years she and Dawn had been friends, she had only gone to Dawn's house once or twice, and never when Jerome was there.

During their years of friendship, Dawn had often confided in Brianna about her father, even revealing how she thought her mother didn't deserve him. Dawn would say, "Just because he drinks doesn't mean he's not sharp." She thought her mother was stupid and weak. "She's not woman enough for Papa," she would say. To Dawn, Papa was a God.

Brianna, too, had fallen for Jerome's charm. He was brilliant, the perfect height, the perfect complexion, and he always smelled good. He hadn't had one drink since he was released from prison. His clothes always fit nicely, and he still had style, like the young guys. His shirts complimented his muscles. His face hadn't matured at all. He had two little strings of gray hair on his left hairline. Other than that, Jerome could easily pass for a man in his late twenties or early thirties. He was also fun.

Brianna and Jerome would often chase each other all over the house. He always had something funny to say, and he was so animated in telling stories. His sex appetite was more than satisfying for Brianna, and she couldn't believe his stamina. He was much more experienced than the younger guys she had previously dated.

There were moments Brianna would lie under Jerome and wish that he could be with her in real life. She wished she could just drop her Bella role altogether and run away with Jerome. She just wanted to stop hiding and really live. She wanted to hug her parents, hang out with her brother Craig, and live in a big house with Jerome.

Sadly, though, such a future was unlikely, given her plan to kill Jerome's pride and joy, Dawn. There was also the fact that Brianna's biological parents knew Jerome from the old neighborhood and would never approve of their relationship.

Brianna had been planning to tell her adoptive parents the truth. She dreaded the day she would have to look into their faces and admit everything. All along, they'd believed her biological parents were monsters. She had grown to love her adoptive parents very much. They'd always treated her and Craig with pure love from the very beginning. It was a very loving upbringing.

Brianna had stayed up crying many nights, missing her mother. She just wanted to run into her arms and kiss her. She missed the pancake Saturdays they'd had every weekend. Her mom had made the best pancakes. They had often played with her make-up and talked about boys. She couldn't just forget where she came from. She wanted her parents back in her life, and getting rid of Dawn was the only way to make that happen.

When Brianna's name changed to Bella, something inside her also changed. She picked up a new identity in place of the sweet girl she had been before. Bella wanted revenge. Bella couldn't be weak like Brianna—look where it got her, after all: It got her raped and almost burned alive. If not for Craig, Brianna would be dead, which was why Craig meant so much to her—even more than her adoptive parents did. She would kill for Craig without blinking twice. His heart was pure, and he was genuinely a kind, sincere person. She felt bad for making him witness the torture she had performed on Damien.

The only reason Brianna had decided to let Damien live was for Craig. She knew if she killed Damien, Craig would never forgive her, and he would always look at her as a monster. That was a risk Brianna wasn't willing to take. So, against her better judgment, she let Damien live.

Brianna laughed to herself, thinking about the fake chip she had placed inside Damien. She hadn't actually put anything inside his shoulder. She had just cut him open, pretended to put something inside his shoulder, and stitched him back up. Damien had been in too much pain to notice the deception.

As she cooked bacon in the kitchen, Brianna sank into a deep daydream in which she tried to figure out how to show Jerome who Dawn really was. She stupidly hoped Papa would see his child for who she was and could somehow forgive Brianna for what she was going to do. She knew it was naive to be so optimistic. Dawn was his child, for god's sake; of course he wouldn't be okay with his girlfriend murdering his daughter. For now, though, Jerome needed to know how evil his child was, and Brianna would figure out the rest as she could.

Bacon grease splattered her arm, burning her and snapping her out of her thoughts. Hurriedly, she scooped up the burned bacon with a spatula and set it on a plate. Over scrambling the eggs in her Versace robe, she may not have known how to cook worth a lick, but at least she looked great trying.

"Baby, come and get these eggs before they get cold!" she yelled to Papa from the kitchen.

"I'm coming. Did you put the coffee on for me?"

"Yes, Jerome. I put the nasty coffee on for you. Anything else, my king?"

"Don't be a smart ass." Papa walked in and picked up his coffee mug. "Where were you yesterday after your meeting?"

"I had to run some errands. Why? Did you miss me?"

There was a sudden edge to his voice. "I noticed your car was in the port, but you weren't here. So, how did you run errands without your car?"

"What's up with the third degree? I used my company's car."

"The Honda?"

"You've seen it?" Brianna was genuinely shocked.

"Yes, Bella. One thing about me is I'm alert. I'm from the streets, and I see and know a lot." He frowned at the blackened bacon. "Did you eat already?"

"No. I was waiting for you. I'm alert, too! I pay attention to everything, that's how I saw your fine ass in the coffee shop."

"Girl, you are green as hell. You are rich and spoiled, and I'm talking about really being from the streets."

"I'm from the streets, too. I wasn't always rich."

"No? You told me you lived in Beverly Hills before you came here—hardly the Bronx."

"Please. You don't even know what kind of things I've been through."

"Like what? Missing a Chanel sale?"

"No, like real-life stuff!" Brianna threw the spatula at the sink and walked away.

Papa seemed genuinely surprised by her outburst. "I'm sorry, baby. I was only joking. I know just because you had money, that doesn't mean life was perfect for you. My bad for judging. Do you want to talk about it?"

"No, let's just have breakfast." She sat down and slammed her fork into her scrambled eggs. "Oh, while we have time to talk, I really want you to get a divorce. Didn't you say your wife had a sister?"

"Yeah, Sheryl. Why?"

"Maybe she knows where her sister is. Have you ever talked to her?"

"No, Sheryl's ass is crazy. She thought I wanted her back in high school." Papa paused and reconsidered. "But you know what, that might not be a bad idea. Dawn and Damien did live with her for a while when I was incarcerated. She might actually know if Sandy was dating someone."

"Well since she had a crush on you, I think I should go with you."

"Awww, my Bella is jealous. That's so cute." Papa pulled Brianna onto his lap.

"I won't say anything when I go with you. I'll just be quiet. It's time for us to get some information, so we can start living freely. I never saw myself as someone's mistress."

"Bella, stop the bullshit. You are not my fucking mistress, and I hate when you talk like that!"

"Calm down, Jerome. I'm just saying." She rubbed his arms to calm him down.

"You can go with me to Sheryl's house, and then we can stop at the hospital to check on Dawn. I'm assuming you don't have any work meetings on a Saturday?"

"Nope, no meetings. I do, however, want to get my nails and toes done, and it's my only day off. So after we go to this sister's house, we can part ways until later."

"Okay, sounds good. I can't wait for you to see Sheryl; you will feel so stupid for acting jealous." Papa laughed.

"Why didn't you eat all your food?" Brianna asked as she got up to start cleaning the kitchen.

"It was a little on the dark side."

"Screw you, Jerome. You better start eating my food because you'll be with me forever!"

"Lord, kill me now!" Papa screamed with laughter. Brianna hit him with the dishrag and ran before he hit her back. Papa grabbed the dish towel and started rolling it up to smack her leg with it. He chased her around the house until they both fell on the carpet, laughing and tussling.

"I love you, Jerome," Brianna said. "No matter what, please always remember that."

Before Papa could answer, his phone began to ring.

"Hello!" he answered, annoyed. "Yeah, wassup?"

"Hey, Jerome. This is Detective Ross. I've been thinking about your lady friend. Do you mind if I ask you a few questions?"

"About what?" Papa awkwardly asked, Brianna's

face inches from his.

"Is she right there with you?"

"Yeah, but we really don't have anything to talk about. I'm trying to keep my life drama-free; you know?"

"I understand," Detective Ross answered, "but I think you'll want to know this. Can we meet later today for lunch? Just you and me?"

"Nah, I'm not okay with that, man."

"I wasn't okay with telling my captain I made a mistake and arrested the wrong man, because of which I had to recant my original statement. I also wasn't okay with being put on desk duty for a month while your trial was going on. But I did it to help you get released, and I'm only asking for a quick meet-up."

"I wasn't okay with being falsely convicted. Don't try that guilty shit with me, man. I shouldn't have been arrested in the first place. Now you want favors? Whatever you think is wrong, I don't want to hear it!" Papa ended the call and angrily tossed his phone aside.

"Damn, who was that?" Brianna asked.

"The detective we ran into the other day," Papa said as he got up off the carpet.

Brianna followed Papa into the kitchen. "What did he want?"

"Some bullshit about the past. Fuck him. Let's get ready."

Brianna felt uneasy, and in her gut she knew that the detective had called about her. She still remembered the confused look on his face when she and Papa got off the elevator. Maybe the detective had recognized her from working on her disappearance case, or from seeing security footage from Dawn's apartment. There was no telling.

They dressed and left for Sheryl's house. The house looked like it had been abandoned for months. The old porch was thick with spider webs, the chairs filled with dust and debris, the doormat covered in old newspapers.

Papa knocked on the door hard. When nothing happened, he knocked again.

"I guess she doesn't live here anymore," he said.

Brianna was peeking through the front window. "No one could possibly live here. This place is a mess."

"You don't know Sheryl. The appearance of this place is not what has me concerned. It's the fact that all her mail is sitting here unbothered."

"Is she dead?" Sheryl yelled as she opened the front door. She was wearing an oversized "Welcome to Orlando" shirt and a pair of holey pants. Her little bit of hair was matted, and her teeth were stained; she looked frail and worn out.

"Is who dead?" Papa said, stepping back from the screen door. "I almost didn't recognize you. I see you lost some weight."

"I know I look good. I've been working out. I'm talking about that little devil of yours." She turned and blew a stream of smoke in Brianna's face. "And who the hell is this?"

"This is my friend Bella," Papa said. "Do you mind if we come in?"

"Hell, yeah, I mind. You come showing up here all these years later and with some skeezer. Anyway, I said I would never let anyone with your blood enter my house again. Pure evil is what you all are."

"Skeezer?" Brianna said coldly.

"Calm down, babe," Papa said.

"Oh, now I'm your babe. I thought I was your friend." She rolled her eyes.

"What the hell do y'all want?" Sheryl interrupted.

"Come on now, Sheryl," Papa said. "Don't be like that. I know Damien is a little off, but I assure you, we come in peace. I have some very important questions to ask you about your sister."

"Who said anything about Damien? Yeah, he's a little asshole, but he's better than that evil little girl you love so much," Sheryl said. She shook her head, dusting Brianna's new pair of Christian Louboutin with ashes.

Papa raised his eyebrows. "What evil little girl, Dawn?"

"Yes, Dawn! Who else? That little bitch took my voice. I was mute for years. I just started talking again a couple weeks ago, so I assumed she died. Is she dead?"

"Sheryl, you must be mistaken. Dawn wouldn't hurt a fly. She definitely couldn't make you mute. Are you sure Damien isn't the one who hurt you?"

"Hell, yeah, I'm sure. Don't get me wrong, Damien is a fucked-up individual too! But he's nothing compared to that devil you call a daughter. I'm kind of scared to say her name because she might come back and haunt me right now." Sheryl took a deep inhale from her newly-lit cigarette as her hand started to shake.

"Why are you shaking? You act like Dawn is a monster or something. I'm confused, and clearly, you are too." Papa stepped off the porch. "Come on, Bella, this is a waste of time."

"The truth hurts, don't it? I'll tell you everything, but next time, how about it's just you and me?" Sheryl's voice had grown soft and seductive as she leaned against the frame of the door.

Brianna couldn't believe what she was hearing. "Are you flirting? Right in front of my face?"

"I don't have to flirt, little girl. How old are you anyway?"

"None of your damn business," Brianna barked.

"Hey, ladies. Let's all be mature here." Papa stared directly into Sheryl's eyes. "Sheryl, will you help me?"

Sheryl opened the screen door and stood to the side.

The house was a disaster. It favored a house from hoarders. It smelled awful, and there was really nowhere to sit. They actually would have been better off sitting on the porch. Sheryl limped to get two extra chairs from the closet, and they sat in the kitchen.

"Thanks," Brianna said as she took the fold-up chair.

"Mmm-hmm," Sheryl sarcastically responded.

Papa sat down. "Thanks, Sheryl. Please tell me everything."

"Well, you know they moved in when you went to jail, and that girl went missing. I think her name was Brittany or something. No, it was Brianna! I remember because they often talked about her, but Sandy would always forbid them to speak of her. Everything went to hell the moment they moved in." Sheryl poured herself a glass of beer from the forty-ounce bottle.

Papa nodded. "Yeah, I remember the girl that went missing. That was so sad. Dawn had a rough time accepting it—the girl was her best friend. What happened after that?"

Brianna's face was furious, but she tried to hide it by looking away. It was the first time she had heard someone refer to her as *the missing girl.*

"Dawn was possessed. She controlled all of us in the house, including Sandy. Every night around midnight, she made evil noises. She terrorized us all. Damien had no idea who Dawn was, but Sandy and I knew. See, in the beginning, Sandy thought it was Damien who hurt that girl, but Sandy saw something Dawn did, but she never said what it was. Out of the blue, Sandy and Damien got really close, and she started avoiding Dawn."

"What? This makes no sense. Why did Sandy leave, and why would she leave her kids with you?"

"That sorry bitch always leaves. She left when our parents got sick, and then had the nerve to be mad they left the house to me. All she ever did was chase after you."

Sheryl took a long swallow of beer. "Anyway, let me finish. Dawn was evil. She pushed me down the steps, punched me in my breast, stomped me, and spat in my mouth. Soon as I screamed, she took my voice somehow. Just like she did to your brother Robby."

"So you telling me Dawn did all that to you? What did you do to her?"

Sheryl lit her third cigarette. "She accused me of some freaky shit, but it was all in her mind. I think she did something to that missing girl, too."

"What makes you say that?" Brianna asked.

"Every time someone mentioned her name, Dawn got annoyed instead of sad. Damien always had a look of regret. Sandy always had a look of sympathy, but Dawn had a look of fulfillment. I can't really explain it."

Brianna had begun pacing. "What kind of person would feel fulfilled? That poor girl was somebody's daughter."

"Sheryl, this sounds like some movie shit," Papa said, annoyed. "Why did Sandy leave?"

"Let her finish talking!" Brianna interjected. "What makes you think Dawn did something to the missing girl?"

"Every time someone talked about her, I could see her eyes turning red. Sandy left because Dawn made her leave. Sandy woke up one morning and made everyone this big breakfast, and then we never saw her again. I'll admit, I wasn't the nicest person to them, but I'm not evil; I'm a good Christian woman."

"Have you heard from Sandy in a while?" Papa said. "I need to find her."

"No. Sandy would call every so often, but then she stopped calling. She also sent them money here for a while, but then that stopped too. I hate to say this, but I think... Oh, never mind." She stubbed her cigarette in the ashtray.

"Say it!" Papa urged, leaning forward in his chair. "Was she dating someone? You can tell me."

"I don't know if she was seeing someone. She would never tell me anyway because I always called her a whore. She stole you from me. I think something bad happened. I don't think she's hiding from you all—I think she's unable to contact you."

"Sheryl, she didn't steal me from you. I was never yours. My friends were supposed to give my number to Sandy, but they pranked me and gave it to you instead.

"So, you didn't love our conversation?"

"I thought I was talking to Sandy for those two days, but the day I came by to pick Sandy up for our date, it was you. I didn't want to hurt your feelings, so I took you out anyway."

"Yeah, yeah, yeah. You know you wanted this." Sheryl rolled her eyes at Brianna.

"So, why do you think Sandy's hurt? Where do you think I can find her?"

"First, is Dawn alive? I'm not sure what she can hear or not. She has powers, and lord knows I don't want that evil girl bothering me."

"Yes, she's alive. I think you are truly mistaken

about her, though. Damien sent me away to prison for a murder I didn't commit—*he's* the manipulative one. Maybe he made you think it was Dawn."

"No, I'm not mistaken, and now that I know she's alive, I'm done talking. She's shown me what she's capable of, and I don't want to be her next victim. She only let me live because they needed a place to stay. Please leave now." Sheryl stood up from her chair.

"Can I please just ask a few more questions?" Papa asked.

"Get the fuck out!" Sheryl yelled as she pointed at the door.

"See, your ass is still crazy. That's why you don't have a man now."

"That may be true, but your daughter is a serial killer, and you are too dumb to know it. I'll be crazy, but I'll be alive. Now, get the hell out of my house!"

Papa and Brianna left. They sat in the car quietly. Brianna glanced through her phone to avoid eye contact. Papa's right leg kept shaking. Brianna gently put her hand on his knee. They were both mentally disturbed, and it was an uncomfortable feeling for them both. Brianna was instantly saddened by the way people talked about the missing girl. It made her think of her parents and all they must've gone through. It broke her heart to think of her mother looking for her every day. She knew her disappearance had destroyed her parents. She also knew her parents would never stop looking.

Papa, on the other hand, was a complete disaster. Everything Sheryl had told him about Dawn disturbed his soul. He immediately started thinking about the anonymous phone call he had received. He wondered if there was some truth to what people were saying. He immediately brushed the idea off. The anonymous call was probably Sheryl.

Brianna and Papa both sat there in deep thought. Papa reflected how every time something went wrong, Dawn always seemed to be involved. He replayed her entire life in his mind.

Meanwhile, Brianna reflected on how Dawn had destroyed her life, and she thought of how she would have to kill her sooner than later.

Papa suddenly pulled the car over to the shoulder of the road, and it jerked them both.

"What the hell, Jerome?" Brianna asked.

"I knew I shouldn't have gone there. Sheryl's a dumb bitch. That shit just ruined my day." He unclasped his seatbelt and slouched in his seat.

Brianna's voice was soft and gentle. "Jerome, maybe you should listen to some of the things she said. Maybe it's things you don't know about your daughter."

"Bella, are you fucking serious? That weirdo just said Dawn is a serial killer. How do I listen to some bullshit like that?"

"Well, Jerome, someone did try to kill her twice in one month. Maybe she is into things you don't know about."

"Fuck! I'm so angry right now, and you are not helping! I've known Dawn her entire life. I held her in my arms for hours when she was born. I think I would know if she was capable of the things Sheryl accused her of doing. I just can't picture it."

"I'm sorry. I didn't particularly care for Sheryl myself, but she did look terrified. For some reason, I believe her."

"So you believe a cigarette-smoking, beer-drinking, beady-head bitch you just met? Over my judgment?"

"Jerome, I think you are so upset because deep down, you think there's some truth to what she's saying. Deep down, you know things were off with Dawn."

"Fuck you, Bella! That was a low blow. You are just like everyone else. Well, Detective Ross had some shit to tell me about you. Did I jump on the bandwagon to hear bad news about you, or did I tell him to go fuck himself? I know all I need to know about you, and I know all I need to know about

Dawn. I don't let people talk down on the people I love. Let's drop it!"

"Okay, fine. I won't say shit else about your daughter. Drop me off at the office; I'd rather work overtime than spend another minute with you."

They rode to Brianna's workplace in silence. It was a fake job; Brianna didn't actually work anywhere. Her adoptive parents still provided all her needs. Papa and Brianna had just had their first big fight, and they both wanted to make up already.

Brianna couldn't believe how much she loved Papa. He drove her crazy, and his aggressive tone turned her on. She really wanted to say, "Drop those clothes and come dig in this pussy with that hard hot dick." Instead, she pretended to still be angry. She got out of his car and slammed the door. After Papa drove away, she walked to a cafe a block away. Brianna realized she hadn't talked to Damien that day, so she decided to give him a call as she sat at a table drinking a cappuccino.

"Hi, Danny Boy! Are you behaving?"

"Hi Brianna—I mean, Bella. Yes, of course I'm behaving! I'm stuck in a hotel! What would I possibly be doing? It kind of feels like I'm back in prison."

"Stop your bitching. I was thinking we may need to move things along a little faster. Dawn will be waking up soon, according to her doctor. I want you to visit her in the hospital."

"And what if my father's there?"

"Right. Actually, I want you to call Dawn at the hospital, just to break the ice. She's in room 706. I'll tell you when to make the call."

"What should I say?"

"When I tell you to call, you will apologize for everything. Tell her your life is messed up without her, and you want to start rebuilding y'all relationship."

"Dawn's not stupid. She'll never believe me."

"*Make* her believe you! I have to go. Keep the phone charged. I'll be calling back shortly."

As Brianna hung up the phone, her waiter arrived. "Would you like a menu, miss?"

"Sure, and can you turn that up, please?" Brianna nodded at the television.

Today in Detroit, we had three shootings at a block party near the Fishkorn neighborhood. No fatalities. Sadly, an African American woman's body was found in the Detroit River. She appeared to have been in the water for quite some time. Police have just released her identity as forty-two-year-old Sandy Scott, mother of the accused Damien Scott. Damien was recently arrested for the murder of Ralph Jones and the disappearance of Brianna Scottsdale. Many of you may remember Brianna Scottsdale. Apparently, she was never found.

Police are asking for anyone with information on the death of Sandy Scott to please contact the Detroit Police Department at 555-992-0000

9
VANESSA'S TURN

I'm sick of sitting in this hotel. The first thing I need to do is find out all I can about this chip Brianna put inside my shoulder. I went to the hotel computer room and searched everything online about bomb chips. I didn't find anything. I did, though, find some information about chips that track a person's location. From my research, bombs were much more complex, and without any wires, it was almost impossible to disarm them. If I was wrong, it would cost me my life. But it was a risk I had to be willing to take, because there was no way I would let Brianna be my master for life.

I started trying to find anything I could about Brianna. I searched her new name, Bella Simms, over a hundred times and came up empty each time. I looked into Craig's adoptive family. On paper, his family appeared perfect. Craig's adoptive father owned a lot of real estate. As I scrolled through the many properties, one particular address stood out: the address of the hotel I was in right then.

The first time we came to this upscale hotel, Craig had said he'd left his wallet. But if his father owned the hotel, he could have gotten us a room. Craig had lied to me. Had he set me up, too, purposely taking me to the cabin to be tortured? Maybe Brianna had something on him and was blackmailing him.

Whatever the reason, I was highly disappointed. It suddenly made sense why they had put me in one of the most luxurious rooms in the entire hotel. They owned the hotel, a fancy room was nothing to them. This information was crucial because it could help me get out of this situation. Imagine allegations of a murderer being held captive at the most luxurious five-star hotel. For now, I'd keep this information to myself. I might need it later to blackmail the Simms family.

When I ran out of things to research, I grew tremendously bored. I literally brushed my teeth ten times, then walked around the hotel admiring the fancy artwork hanging on the walls. I started random conversations with the front desk staff. It sickened me to pretend I cared about their grandkids or whatever topic they spoke of. I enjoyed the five-star meals, which were always freshly cooked and packed with flavor.

Around Happy Hour, the bar area became a bit interesting. They served free house drinks for all the guests. I didn't waste any time, drinking only the best and charging it to the fancy room that was my prison. After a while, I decided to get dressed and go to the lounge area.

I hadn't woken up thinking that day would be much different than the day before, but nothing could be further from the truth. My life would drastically change after that day, and I would never be the same human being again. We are constantly changing without knowing it. Our cells are rejuvenating, our skin is peeling, and change is inevitable. This change would be for the worst. The last time I'd undergone a significant change was when Mr. Ralph died. I felt mentally confused and bitter. Now something similar was happening.

I sat at the bar's marbled countertop and ordered a forty-dollar shot of Don Julio 1942. Glancing around the room, I noticed a stunning woman sitting alone at the end of the bar, watching television. It was the same attractive woman I had seen when I was here with Craig the last time. I couldn't believe she was still here as a guest. I hadn't expected to ever see her again.

As I watched, she slid her hair behind her ear. It instantly turned me on—not sexually, but in some kind of pleasing way that made my heart smile. Something about the motion of moving hair in a sensual way excited me. I studied her ear, which appeared to have a two-carat diamond stud in it. She flashed a set of perfect teeth at the bartender, and I instantly needed to know who she was.

I had to meet her this time. I couldn't let her slip away again. I sent her a drink and put it on my room tab. I looked away, staring at the opposite end of the bar, where a fat white guy with a belly popping out of his shirt was loudly sharing his opinion about some sports team. I sat quietly, observing the room.

Suddenly my view of the woman was blocked by a handsome black man who pulled out a chair to sit next to me. He had a fresh haircut and wore a suit tailored to perfection. I couldn't tell if he was gay, bisexual, or just effeminate. I knew after a quick conversation that his sexuality would be revealed to me. Homosexual men have our own language. We can spot each other by body language, word choice, and conversation.

"Is this seat taken?" the tall, handsome guy asked. I instantly noticed his wedding ring.

"Now it is," I responded.

"Thanks, man." He loosened his tie. "What brings you here?"

"I'm here to do a job for a partner," I simply responded. I was already annoyed that he was married, and now he appeared to be a talker as well.

"I'm in charge of all the Sun's Banks on this coast. It's really a pain in my ass. Have to fly all around to babysit fucking idiots. People can't do the most simple shit." He lifted his hand to flag down the bartender.

"What are you drinking?" I asked. "It's on me." I looked toward the end of the bar to ensure the mysterious woman hadn't left. I was relieved to see she was still there, but now someone was sitting next to her, and he partially blocked my view.

"Thanks, man. The next one is on me." He turned to the bartender. "I'll take a double shot of crown royal and a club soda."

The handsome young bank manager wasted no time telling me his whole life story, including all the cute anecdotes of his snotty-nosed kids. I had no interest in his life, and I didn't even bother to ask his name. His voice was starting to make me angry, and I could feel myself losing control.

"You stuck-up slut!" I heard a man yell at the end of the bar. The entire lounge looked in his direction.

"Sir," the bartender said, "you need to leave. We don't talk to women like that around here!"

"Screw you and her!" he yelled back.

"What's the problem?" I asked, now standing in front of the stunning woman who appeared terrified by the guy's aggression.

"You about to be my problem if you don't mind your got damn business. I asked that stuck-up skank for her number after buying her three drinks." He belched before continuing. "She had the nerve to tell me she doesn't give out her number, but she sure didn't mind drinking all my damn money up!"

"It's not that serious," the woman said. "You are being extremely disrespectful. I guess you Detroit men were raised by wolves. Here's a hundred dollars—that should cover you and my drinks." The woman threw several bills at him.

The guy raised his hand to smack her. I caught his hand and punched him with all my might. Sadly, he didn't fall on the floor like in the movies, but before he could hit me back, the staff dragged him out.

"Thank you so much!" the woman said to me. "He was such an asshole. I'm Vanessa, by the way. Please have a seat—I can at least buy you a drink."

She sat back in her seat and elegantly crossed her legs. I was intrigued by her style. She was relaxed enough to allow her shirt to hang effortlessly off her shoulder, but classy enough to only show a peek of cleavage.

"Only if I can give you my number," I said as I pulled a chair out. "That's the going rate for a drink these days."

She laughed, then her smile faded as she got a good look at me. I had forgotten how bad I looked. It wasn't until she frowned with concern that I remembered the bruises Brianna had left when she pistol-whipped me.

"I'm sorry to ask," she said, "but I'm curious. What happened to your face? You appear to be a handsome guy under those scars. Sorry if I'm intruding." She picked up her glass and took a sip, waiting for me to answer.

"I was on the wrong side of town to meet a client, and I got mugged by a gang. They beat me pretty bad, which is why I was happy the hotel staff came to get that guy before things got too rough. I'm really not capable of defending myself right now—or anyone else, for that matter."

"And still you risked another beatdown for little ole me. That deserves another drink." There was a slight slur to Vanessa's voice.

"Actually, I've already hit my limit. My father was a horrible alcoholic, so drinking is not my thing."

"Well, thanks for the drink you got me earlier. I never made eye contact with you to say thanks."

"No problem. I forgot to introduce myself. I'm Damien. I thought you were the prettiest lady in here, and I said when I came to the bar, I would buy the most attractive woman a drink as soon as I sat down. I scoured the room, and you were the lucky winner."

I laughed. She laughed, too. She smelled delightful, like a bath of roses. Her floral perfume wasn't too strong or too weak. It was just right.

Looking at the empty glasses on the bar's countertop, she said, "I probably should've stopped three drinks ago, but I lost the biggest deal of my career, so what the hell. I hate Detroit and will be happy as hell to catch my flight out of here tomorrow evening."

"That makes me sad—it means I won't see you again." I pretended to pout.

"Oh, stop it. I'm actually glad we had this talk. It's surely been entertaining." Vanessa smirked as she took another sip of her drink.

I could tell she was feeling it because a small drop of alcohol missed her lip and fell onto her shirt. Usually, such sloppiness would be a turn-off, but with her, it was actually cute.

I didn't know what my intentions were with this woman. Initially, I was just bored and drawn to her. I didn't know what I would do if I was to get her in my room. Would I rape her or just let her be? Maybe I could be normal and just allow her to fall asleep on my bed and never speak to her again.

My mind raced, thinking of future acts. Vanessa continued to talk, and I fell into a deep daydream. I had no idea what she was saying; I just sat back and admired how her lips moved with her perfect shade of dark red lipstick. I watched her put her hair behind her ear every time it fell out of place. That turned me on. I've always been infatuated with a woman's hair. I admired how this woman knew exactly when her hair was out of place and fixed it immediately. It was pure class in my eyes. I had tried to teach Dawn that kind of class, but she never got it. I will never forget the look on Vanessa's face when the conversation went to hell.

"That's so sad what happened to that lady," she said, sipping her vodka and cranberry "It's some crazy people out here."

"What lady?" I asked.

"The lady that's been all over the news. Her body was found in the Detroit River. I just hate to see our black women dying. It sickens me." Vanessa shook her head sadly.

"Dag, that is sad. You never know who people

are, you know?" I shook my head back at her.

"I'm safe with you, though, right?" Vanessa grinned, batting her eyelashes.

"Well, of course. I'm a gentleman, and I'm just enjoying your company—nothing more." Oddly enough, this was the truth.

"There she goes," Vanessa said, focused on the television. "That's the woman." She glanced at the bartender. "Sir, you can cut that up, please?" She leaned forward eagerly.

I looked up, and that's when I saw my beautiful mother's face plastered across the evening news. My heart dropped; it may have even skipped a few beats. It felt like someone had reached inside my chest and squeezed my heart. The pain was worse than anything I had ever felt before.

All of a sudden, I felt heavy. I didn't know if the barstool could hold me up. The television flashed three pictures of Mama and then finally a picture of me. They said I was the son of the victim, who had been convicted of murder and the disappearance of Brianna.

I felt Vanessa's eyes on me. She was staring at me like I was a monster, and so were a few other people in the lounge area. I was exposed, and tears filled my eyes for the loss of my mother. I had lost the only person who had truly loved me. It was an awkward silence, and I couldn't escape the room fast enough.

"Sorry for the loss of your mother," she said in a cautious, fearful tone. "I can tell by the look on your face that you are just finding out. For that, I'm so sorry. On the other hand, please don't say anything else to me."

"I didn't do those things. I was falsely convicted."

"Please, don't. Just don't. I guess I now know what really happened to your face." Vanessa rose and walked away.

I wanted to butcher her right there. Someone needed to feel my pain. How insensitive that bitch was. I had just lost my mother.

I got up to see what room she was in. I knew she wasn't a smart target because everyone had seen me talking to her and even getting into a bar fight for her. I clearly wasn't thinking, though, because I continued to follow her. She eventually turned around and saw me. Before I could say anything, she quickly pressed the elevator button and stepped through the doors, which shut behind her after a few moments. I watched the floors light up, until finally it stopped on the eleventh floor. I rushed to grab the next elevator and unexpectedly bumped into Craig.

"What are you doing here?" I demanded.

"I'm here for you. I just heard about your mother, and I rushed right over. Are you okay?" He moved close to me, but not close enough to look suspicious or attracted to me.

"Hell no, I'm not okay. I was just about to murder someone, and you just ruined it. Like you ruin everything." I was so overwhelmed, I didn't even realize what I was saying.

"About to murder someone. Good one." He laughed nervously. "Damien, you need to know I didn't have anything to do with what Bella did to you, I'd never seen that side of her before."

"I don't believe you," I answered coldly. "I think you knew Brianna would be there, and I can't trust you. Whatever we had between us before is done. You are dead to me, just like my mother."

"Damn! But I've been here for you through everything. You were accused of murdering my father, kidnapping Bella, and even rape. I still came to check on you. No matter what people said about you, I still loved you."

"That was always your biggest mistake. You loved a monster. I am brutal, and I am dangerous. I am the definition of evil. Now that I know that the one person who truly loved me is gone, I am capable of the unthinkable." I snorted. "If you were smart, you would leave now."

"Don't say that. I can still see the good in you— there's still that light in your eyes."

"If you see the light in my eyes, then you are blind. You are clearly deaf or retarded. I just told you who I really am, and you still have hope there's light in my eyes. I'm ruthless. I tried to behave and look at what it got me: you played me, I got tortured by a bitch, I got set up by your sister, and my mother is dead."

"Damien, you are grieving, and you have every right to be upset. But I know you." He reached for my arm.

I jerked him toward me. "Look in my eyes!"

Craig glanced around the hotel to see whether anyone was watching—afraid they'd report back to his adoptive father, probably. "I don't have to. I know what your eyes look like." He looked everywhere but at me.

"Look into my fucking eyes!" I yelled. A few of the guests turned around. They had just gotten off the elevator where we stood. Craig looked into my eyes, and after a few seconds, I released his arm. He looked terrified. I saw his right hand shaking as he stood there silent, physically unable to speak.

"I'm sorry I bothered you, Damien," he murmured, lowering his head. "I'll tell Bella to call this thing off. Please just stay away from us. If there was ever anything between us, just please stay away."

"I will promise no such thing! I will burn your entire ship down. There will be no witnesses. No one is safe. Just so you know, Craig, I found out some interesting details about your family."

Craig hurried away, "Leave my family out of this!"

"I always planned on leaving you alive—that is, until—oh never mind." I paused. "I hope you didn't forget your wallet this time," I said as I hit the elevator button for the top floor.

"What about my wallet?" Craig turned to ask.

"Yes, your wallet. You didn't need one that night. Your family owns this place. So, that means you took me to the cabin to set me up, not to get a fucking wallet. But anyway, thanks for putting me in the Penthouse Suite." I stepped onto the elevator.

Craig left in a panic. Soon after entering the elevator, I hit the emergency stop button and fell to the floor. I balled up in a fetal position and cried. I had lost my mother, and nothing would bring her back, so I let myself feel the pain. I screamed and cried. The pain was unbearable, and my body couldn't wait to inflict this pain on others. At that moment, I decided I had nothing to live for. It was time to be Damien again.

I would tear their motherfucking empire down. I would torture and kill everyone responsible for my pain. No one would be exempt. I would teach them to fear me. They were officially living on borrowed time. I always won in the end, but this was just the beginning.

I watched a teardrop fall to the elevator floor, and something inside me snapped. That was the last tear I would cry for Mama—or for anyone else, for that matter. I couldn't be weak.

I released the emergency latch, and the elevator began moving again. Unexpectedly, the elevator stopped on the eleventh floor. The doors opened, and there she stood with her long legs and Louis Vuitton luggage. She looked afraid. Her black mascara was running as if she had been crying. Her eyes were big and frightened, and her body appeared to be frozen as she stared wide-eyed into my face. Her jacket was halfway on, hanging recklessly off her shoulder, allowing just a peek of skin to show. Her purse was unzipped, and she appeared flustered. It was as if Vanessa had seen a ghost.

Suddenly she turned to run. I grabbed her long hair and dragged her onto the elevator. She screamed. I slapped her hard, spit flying out of her mouth and landing on my shoulder. I smiled.

Vanessa began to swing baby punches, and I took them all and laughed. I accidentally hit the open button on the elevator door, and she tried to run out. I threw her across the elevator floor, snatched her fancy luggage, and threw it at her. I stood tall as the elevator door shut. Vanessa scrambled on the floor, trying to gain her balance, and I let her.

I was unbothered by her screaming and punching. The next stop was the penthouse. What I loved most about the penthouse was the complete privacy. There was only one room at the top.

Poor Vanessa was always taking drinks from the wrong men, apparently. It was too late for her to learn her lesson, though, because this stop would be her last.

(*ding: Penthouse Suite*)

10
CHEATING DEATH

"I'm alive, bitches," was Dawn's first thought when she opened her eyes. She had prayed for this moment when the bullet punctured her skull. She had told God that if he allowed her to open her eyes, she would tell the truth about everything.

She had lied, though. In her mind, God had created her, so he knew she was a rotten apple. Fuck eating the forbidden apple—Dawn *was* the toxic apple.

Her throat was parched, and she felt partially there and partially gone. Her thoughts were fumbled by chaos. Her body was non-responsive. She couldn't feel anything, but she heard the heart monitor beeping, pumping fake oxygen into the frail lungs that had suffered a gunshot wound—a gunshot wound from someone Dawn had once envied. Dawn had envied Brianna for her pink room, for being an only child with well-off parents. Funny, how others' lives often looked perfect on the outside.

Dawn's cold heart was filled with hate. She decided to torture every person who crossed her. Before her surprise visit from Brianna, Damien was Dawn's primary target. But that pretty bitch Brianna had just won first place.

Dawn thought to herself, *"She should have blown my head completely off my neck to ensure I was dead."* She couldn't believe God actually let her blink her eyes— the same eyes, according to Damien, that held her truth.

Dawn had felt dead long before the first bullet ripped through her skin. *"How ridiculous is it that skin is our biggest organ, and yet, everything that can harm us can break through it. And I'm the one fucked up?"*

She felt delirious and tired. She had been using her mental strength to create nightmares for everyone the moment she was conscious enough to concentrate.

She replayed the moments before and after she had gotten shot. She remembered sitting on her white Italian leather sofa and feeling the cold leather on her legs, a feeling she hated. She always put a blanket on the couch before sitting on it. Dawn remembered how Brianna's phone had rung, but she had refused to answer it. Lastly, she remembered the knock on the door, the last sound before the gunshots. She thought she remembered hearing Craig's voice as she lay there dying, but she may have imagined it.

Now that she'd had another near-death experience, she felt unafraid of death. She welcomed it. She vowed to kill every last one of them, and she was prepared to die too. She decided not to stop until no one was breathing. She finally hit the call button, closed her eyes, and waited.

"Someone page Dr. Smidget!" a nurse yelled. "Dawn, can you hear me? Don't speak, just nod your head."

"I can speak," Dawn lightly responded.

"I can't believe it!" Dr. Smidget said, a big smile on his face as he entered the hospital room. "You came around again! I've been taking care of you every day in your coma state. I feel pretty lucky to have saved your life twice."

"Thank God I always have you to bring me back," Dawn said, smiling. "Am I okay? I can barely feel anything."

"Well, you are either the unluckiest patient I've ever had, or someone is really trying to kill you. You were shot twice, once to the head and once to the chest. We were able to remove both bullets. Luckily the bullet didn't travel to your heart, but it did destroy some of your lung tissue. For now, try not to talk too much."

"I feel so weak. Has my father been here?" Dawn rubbed her head to feel how much hair she had left.

"Every day! You are lucky to have such a dedicated dad—he was here just yesterday with his lady friend. He'll be thrilled to hear you're awake."

"Lady friend? What does she look like?"

"She's a pretty one, a little younger than your dad, but they seem really happy," Dr. Smidget said as he listened to Dawn's breathing with his stethoscope.

"I wonder if it was my mom. Do you happen to know the woman's name?"

"Her name was…um…let me think. It's on the tip of my tongue. Oh yeah, Bella. Her name was Bella." He hit her knee to check Dawn's reflexes.

"Interesting," Dawn answered. "I didn't know my father knew anyone named Bella. Am I safe? Has the person who did this to me been arrested?"

"Detective Ross provided an officer at your door for twenty-four-hour surveillance. He informed me to call him the moment you woke up; I had a nurse contact him already. Dawn, just please try to relax. Unfortunately, we can't let your father see you until

Detective Ross questions you first, but I will let him know you pulled through. For now, let's just try to keep you alive, okay?" He smiled as he wrote "Welcome back AGAIN" on the board.

Dawn felt her heart pumping uncontrollably as she sat there waiting for Detective Ross. She wasn't nervous but impatient. Unlike the last time Dawn was in the hospital after her booty-loving brother threw her down a mountain, this time she wanted to show she was healed. She wanted to be discharged right away. No faking amnesia or prolonging the process.

She knew Papa was worried, and she wanted to see him just so he could breathe again. Papa loved her more than Dawn could ever love him, which was always comforting for her.

It wasn't long before Detective Ross entered Dawn's hospital room. She had seen him a few times at Papa's re-trial, and he always looked the same. There he was, still slinky in his old-fashioned brown suit. This time he had on a Kangol hat, which didn't match his suit. It was a weird fashion statement and instantly threw her off.

"Little Ms. Dawn, I'm so happy to see your eyes open," Detective Ross said. "How are you?"

"I've been better. Did you arrest whoever did this to me?"

"We need your help with that. We have no idea who did this to you. We took fingerprints from your apartment, but the analysis may take weeks."

"I heard a noise while I was in the shower. I grabbed a towel, and someone knocked me down, blindfolded me, and dragged me to the couch." Tears filled Dawn's eyes as she recounted the attack.

Detective Ross handed her a tissue. "So sorry this happened to you. How many people do you think it was?"

"Maybe two, but I'm really not sure. I do remember one thing that has really bothered me."

"What is it, Dawn? Even the smallest of details will help. Do you know what they were looking for? We noticed your place had been searched."

"I don't know what they were looking for, but I saw something strange." Dawn paused, breathing heavily. "I saw my fiancé Craig's shoes, and I also smelled his cologne. He wears Calvin Klein, and I smelled it soon as they threw me on the sofa."

Detective Ross scribbled something on his notepad. "Interesting. What do you know about Craig and his family?"

"Craig's family comes from money, but other than that, I don't know. He has a sister that I never met, and he rarely talks about her." Dawn shrugged.

"Where is Craig now?"

SUNNI T. CONNOR

"I'm not sure."

"Do you think he would hurt you? He's your fiancé, right?"

"Yes, we were engaged. Craig has been acting weird lately, though. Come to think of it, he purchased an insurance policy for me once he knew I was pregnant. But I doubt he could be so cold as to do this."

"You were pregnant? How did Craig feel about it? Sorry for your loss." Detective Ross lowered his hat.

"Thanks. He didn't know I had lost the baby. He honestly didn't want a child. He wanted to focus on his career, but we were working through it. To be honest, I haven't seen him since we were in the mountains."

"Wait, so he hasn't checked on you since the mountain incident? What's his full name?"

"His name is Craig Simms. If Craig did this to me, what would happen to him? I still love him."

Detective Ross's pen scratched at the pad. "I can't say for sure, but likely he will be arrested. I need to question him. Please write down any addresses where you think he might be. You sure you don't have more to tell me? I promise I will protect you, but you have to tell me what's going on."

"This is hard. I'm still trying to process everything. I don't understand why this is happening. I think I should speak up since it's Craig's second attempt. My memory recently returned, and I remembered Craig pushing me off the mountain. The flashbacks were so real. To be honest, I was going to confront Craig myself, and I didn't know what I would do next." Dawn did her best to keep a straight face.

"Why would he push you off a mountain? Did you both have a fight?"

"I found out he was sleeping with Damien. He wouldn't get his inheritance if his family knew he was involved with a man, so we argued, and he pushed me." Her voice trailed off as she began to sob.

"Damien is gay? Can you remember anything else? We can place him at the scene for the mountain attempt, and that's enough to arrest him, but any other details from the shooting?"

"He shot me! It was Craig. What a relief to finally say it aloud. Craig shot me. The blindfold wasn't completely dark, and I saw his face. Sorry I didn't tell you this initially, but I'm a little traumatized and didn't want my father to know. He will kill him and go back to jail. Please don't tell my father, Detective Ross."

"Thanks for opening up, Dawn. I won't tell your dad. That's your decision. But I don't understand why you are just telling me this now. Why are you protecting a man who tried to kill you twice?"

"Love. Love is why. Do you love someone, Detective Ross? Love will make you do the dumbest things."

"I had one woman I loved, and she was murdered, which is why I'm so big on solving my cases. I sympathize with you, but Craig may try to contact you. It might be a good idea for us to keep an eye on your apartment for a few days."

"I agree. Thanks for everything." She smiled, trying to communicate the gratitude she didn't feel.

"It's my job. Just one more question, but it's not related to the crime. What do you know about your father's girlfriend, Bella?"

"I haven't met her yet. I didn't even know he had a girlfriend. Why?" Dawn raised her eyebrows.

"No reason. I was just curious. Did she remind you of…" He shook his head. "Nevermind. You get some rest. I'll allow your dad to come in now. I know he is anxious to see you. Oh, yeah, just as a heads up, Damien was released on bail. Be careful. I know he loves you, but just be careful. I'm also so sorry about your mother."

Dawn didn't say anything as Detective Ross left. She didn't even question why he had mentioned her mother.

Dawn was discharged two days later. She sat in her kitchen on one of the tall bar stools, which Craig had loved but Dawn hated. She drank apple juice as she picked over her eggs. She still didn't have an appetite.

She smiled with joy, knowing she had begun the process to set up Craig to take the blame for her shooting. She felt her duty was almost done with him. She wanted him to get raped and tortured in jail. Dawn thought jail would be an excellent punishment for Craig sticking his slimy penis in Damien.

Since the detectives would be watching Dawn's house, she just needed a way to get Craig to come and see her. Why not help the detectives arrest Craig? She thought back on what Craig had enjoyed most while they were dating: working out at the gym. She dialed Craig's number, which she still knew by heart.

"Hello, Craig. I'm sure you are surprised to hear from me. Do you have a moment to talk?"

"I am surprised. I thought you were...never mind. I'm happy you pulled through. Honestly, Dawn, I'm not sure what you want, but I don't have the energy for this right now. I'm glad you are alive, but I'm not sure what you want from me."

"Craig, throughout all of this, you have treated me the worst. I was carrying your child, but you stabbed me in the back by sleeping with my brother, and you didn't even come to see me in the hospital. I knew I would never take you back after seeing you with

Damien, but we were engaged, and I do still love you."

Dawn smirked in the mirror as she applied her mascara. Everything took forever, so she had to start her makeup hours before she intended to leave out.

"Dawn, I don't believe for one moment you thought about me. I don't know what you're up to, but I won't fall for it."

"What I'm up to?" Dawn asked innocently as she shaped her eyebrows. "Do you think I can just throw away years of my life that I shared with you? I am still human despite what everyone may say. I'm sure Damien put a lot of junk in your head, but it's not true."

She noticed her vanity mirror was dirty, so she stood up to get some Windex.

"I don't want to talk about Damien," Craig said. "I'm assuming you lost the baby, and yes, I've heard horrible things about you."

"Yes, our baby is gone. Thanks to…never mind. I don't want to talk about that right now. Whatever Damien told you is not true; whatever anyone has said is not true. Damien is the real devil, and he can make me look evil, but it's actually him. Do you believe me?"

"No! I don't believe you," Craig said sternly.

"Well, let me ask you this," she said, putting on

the red lipstick she knew Craig liked. "Did I ever do anything to you? Did I ever hurt you? Did I ever haunt you or try to kill you? I had years to torture you if that's who I truly was. Did I ever do any of those things to you?"

"What does that matter now?" Craig asked in a weak voice, as if he had lost his confidence.

"It means Damien is lying! Do you think Damien is capable of love? He hurt you, killed your father, and did something to that missing girl. Did you know that, as a kid, Damien dressed like me sometimes? We are strangely identical, and he used that to his advantage. He once cut off all my hair so he could pretend to be me. I can tell by your silence, you are thinking about something you know he did that was evil."

Craig's voice was soft and full of regret. "I think I do believe you. I've seen evil in Damien's eyes, and it was like the real-life devil was right in front of me. I'm sorry everyone thinks it's you."

Dawn threw on her wig and began brushing it slowly. "I'm sorry he made you love me. I'm sorry he set us up just to torture me. He's sick, you know?"

"Yeah, I know now. I do wonder what our baby would've looked like. How are you, Dawn? Are you recovering okay? I've actually missed your voice. Everything has been so crazy."

He was finally letting his guard down. *About damn time,* Dawn thought.

"No, I'm not okay," Dawn answered. "I actually called because I need your help. I have no one else to call. My mom died, you know? I've been severely depressed. I just need you to help me with my physical therapy. I need to learn how to use my limbs again. The shooting really screwed me up."

"I'm so sorry about your mom. My heart went out to you both as soon as I heard. I felt bad for your dad, too; I know he really loved her." He paused, hesitating. "So, you just need me to help you work your muscles?"

"Yes. I already have a treatment plan, but I'm a little afraid to leave my house. I'm still a little traumatized by the shooting. Do you think you can help me? We can also talk when you get here and make everything right."

"Yeah, I'll help you. We need closure. How often will you need me?"

"For now, just twice a week. As far as I'm concerned, all is forgiven. Having a near-death experience has truly changed me. I'm still upset about you and Damien, but I know he can be very manipulative. I'm just happy to be alive at this point. Can you come now?" she used that sweet, charming voice she knew Craig couldn't deny.

"Sure. I can be on my way. Hopefully, we can fix things."

"I hope so as well. Oh yeah, the strangest thing happened after I got shot. I thought I heard your voice, and I knew I had to forgive you if I ever woke up because my subconscious made me think of you in my last moments. It was weird."

"That is strange. You thought you heard my voice? After you got shot?" Craig sounded genuinely surprised.

"Yup, clear as day. The doctor said I was probably hallucinating. Anyway, I'll see you soon. How long are you thinking?"

"I have to make a few calls, but I can be there within an hour."

"Thanks again, Craig. I'll see you soon."

Craig immediately hung up and called Bella, but she didn't answer. He sat and thought for a moment, then he called again and left a voicemail.

Dawn had seemed authentic, and she had made some valid points. She had never done anything evil to Craig over the years. She had actually been pretty good to him. Craig then thought of Damien and all the evil he had done. He couldn't believe he was in love with such a monster.

Craig couldn't forget that demonic look in Damien's eyes. Just thinking about it scared him. He also thought about all Bella had told him about Dawn. He questioned whether Bella had been mistaken; maybe she had been wrong all along.

If Damien was dressing like Dawn, perhaps he was the one who choked Bella out. Damien was the one who raped her. He was the one jealous of their friendship.

Against his instincts, he decided to go over to Dawn's house. If nothing else, he could make things right with Dawn, and Bella could live a normal life.

He stopped at a gas station and looked at the sky. It was so beautiful. He thought of the times he and Bella had gone camping, and how they would look at the sky and try to count the stars.

Craig decided he would try to convince Bella to just leave. There was too much drama. He thought maybe they could escape both Dawn and Damien and start over.

He put the gas pump back in the holder and sniffed the air. It was the smell of freedom. It was the smell of choice.

Craig drove to Dawn's house, walked to her door, and nervously rang the bell. She opened the door, entirely made up in an all-black outfit. Craig knew at that moment, he wasn't there to massage her legs and help her get muscle strength back. He knew he had made a horrible mistake.

Dawn smiled the most vicious, evil smile Craig

had ever seen. He then saw the same look he had seen in Damien's eyes, but before he could walk away, Dawn screamed an excruciating scream. It was horrific, and it echoed through the apartment building.

"Help! Somebody, please. Help me! He's trying to kill me again. Please! Help! He has a knife. Oh my God. Please don't hurt me, Craig. Please!"

A uniformed officer stepped into view. "Sir, get down on the floor! Put your hands where I can see them!"

"I don't have anything!" Craig pleaded. "I didn't do anything. I tried to move, but it was like I was stuck. She made me stand still like a statue. She put the knife in my hand; she's crazy!" He lifted his hands, still holding the knife.

"Craig, get on the floor and drop the knife," Detective Ross ordered. "Don't make me say it again!"

By coincidence, Detective Ross had arrived at Dawn's house to question her about Bella at the same time as Craig.

Craig dropped the knife. "Okay, okay. Please don't shoot. I'm getting down. I'm getting down slowly. I didn't hurt her. I would never hurt a woman—or anyone, for that matter. She is insane." He knelt and interlaced his hands behind his back.

"If she's crazy, then why are you here?" Detective Ross asked as he lifted Craig to his feet and proceeded to walk him away.

"I came here to make it right. I was trying to make it right. Dawn, don't do this. I know there's some good in you somewhere, and you know I don't deserve this."

"Thanks, Detective Ross, for keeping your word," Dawn said with a deep sigh of relief. "I can finally get some sleep tonight, and I feel safe for the first time in a long time."

She shut her apartment door and whispered to herself, *"One down, two more to go. I'm back, bitches!"*

11

CRAIG'S TURN

Brianna sat in a marble hot tub surrounded by candles. A nice bath was the only thing that allowed her to relax. She felt off, and she missed Jerome. She hadn't talked to Jerome since they'd left Sheryl's and argued about Dawn. She was exhausted from the drama.

She couldn't believe someone had murdered Jerome's wife. She had actually liked Mrs. Sandy – that was what Brianna used to call her – when she was a child. She had always told Dawn how beautiful her mother was, and now she was dead. It made Brianna wonder what kind of evil really resided in this family.

Maybe she was in over her head, trying to get revenge. Maybe she should have stayed in hiding. It was her biological family that had made her come out into the open. She missed them so much. She had finally received a call a few weeks ago from a private detective who had found her mom. Sadly, her dad divorced her mom shortly after Brianna went missing. Maybe he couldn't handle the pressure, or maybe having a missing daughter was too much. People stay together all the time for their kids.

Brianna wondered whether Jerome knew about Sandy's death. She wanted to call him, but he still wasn't talking to her. She decided to stop thinking and just lay her head back. Just as she closed her eyes, however, her phone rang.

"Bella!" Papa said. "I'm glad you answered. I know I've been an ass. I'm sorry. I miss you, and I couldn't take being without you another day."

Brianna sat up in the tub. "Yes, you were an ass! But I miss you, too."

"I have good news."

Brianna pressed the speaker button and placed her phone on the edge of the tub so she could lather her long legs with soap. "Well, what is it? I like to hear the good stuff."

"Dawn woke up two days ago! She can talk and everything! I can't believe it. I know you probably thought I was staying out, but I've been at Dawn's helping her recover.

"Oh, that's where you've been?" Brianna asked nervously, the thought of Dawn being alive made her heart pump rapidly.

"I left this morning—well, she kind of put me out." Papa laughed. "I was thinking today about how short life is. Too short not to introduce the two ladies of my life." He paused, waiting. "Aren't you going to say something?"

"I'm happy she pulled through. But I can't be phony, Jerome. The things her aunt said still have me a little bothered, but if you love her, so will I. Let's have dinner at the house tomorrow night. Let me get to know her for myself. Sound good?"

"Hell yeah—well, if Dawn's up to it, but I'm sure she will be. I can't wait to come home tonight. Dawn's couch is hard as hell." Papa laughed. Brianna immediately pictured Dawn's couch. Dawn had been sitting there before Brianna pulled the trigger.

"Have you watched the news?" Brianna asked to change the subject.

"You know I hate the news. It's a bunch of bad stuff going on. Too negative. Dawn doesn't watch it either. Why you ask?"

"Well, have you talked to Detective Ross or Damien?"

"No! Fuck them both. Detective Ross has been calling me every day like we buddies or some shit. Dawn showed me how to block him, so I blocked his ass. Damien knows not to call me. Stop beating around the bush, Bella, what's up?"

"I hate to be the one to tell you, but…" Brianna froze and took a deep breath.

"But what, baby?"

"Your wife Sandy was murdered and found in the Detroit River; it's all over the news. I thought you knew, and I thought maybe that's why you were staying away from me this long. Like maybe you needed to grieve or something."

"What? Oh my God. No! What happened to her?" Papa's voice cracked and Brianna could hear him sniffling.

"I'm sorry I had to be the one to tell you. I know you always loved her, and maybe that's why Detective Ross kept calling. I'm so sorry, Jerome."

"Shit. I can't tell Dawn, not yet anyway. She's too fragile right now. We can still have dinner tomorrow night, and I'll talk to her. I feel horrible. I did love that woman. Bella, promise me something."

"What is it?" she asked as she lathered the rag.

"Promise me you will let me feel my emotions. I was with Sandy most of my life. This will not take away from what we have, but I have to be honest, this will be hard."

"Jerome, I genuinely love you. Take as much time as you need, and I will let you grieve without feeling resentment. I can't wait to cuddle tonight. See you soon. Love you."

"I love you too, Bella. Damn, I can't believe this. I'm going to take a long ride to clear my mind, and I'll be home in a few hours."

Papa ended the call.

Brianna couldn't read Jerome. She wondered if Dawn had told him that Brianna had shot her, but Jerome wouldn't know Brianna was Bella. They never took pictures together because Jerome hated pictures, and Brianna was smart enough to never reveal her identity. She had been trained since she was a child to hide Brianna. So even if Dawn did tell Papa who shot her, Bella would be safe.

Craig had called about three times while she was on the phone with Jerome. She really just wanted to finish her relaxing bath, but that seemed impossible. Craig had been highly annoying since he saw Brianna torture Damien. All he talked about was Damien, and how this was wrong, and that was wrong. It made Brianna ignore his calls. He never called three times in a row, though, so maybe it was important.

She called her voicemail and listened.

"Bella. This is Craig. You really need to answer your phone. We have to call this thing off with Damien. He's not who I thought he was. I saw something that I can't explain over the phone, just please trust me. We have to let it go. It's no longer about my love for him. I understand now. He's dangerous, Bella. I'm on my way to fix things with Dawn. We can finally move forward. I'll tell her that she will never hear from us again, and in return, we will leave Detroit. Let's just move away or something. We always hated the cold anyway. What about California? You always talked about moving there one day. I love you; please call me back."

After Brianna listened to the voicemail, she jumped out of the tub, grabbed a towel, quickly blew out the candles, and rushed to her room to get dressed. She called Craig multiple times and kept getting the voicemail. She hurriedly called Damien as she fumbled through her panty drawer looking for underwear.

"Yeah?" he answered gruffly.

Brianna squeezed into a pair of jeans. "We are changing the plans. I need you to meet me at this address tomorrow night."

"Ard," he nonchalantly answered.

"I don't like your attitude. You do know I still own your bitch ass, right? You don't want to fuck with me today. Have your ass there tomorrow night. I'll text the location soon. And stay the fuck away from Craig. Do you understand me?"

"Whatever you say," Damien responded with no emotion.

"That's right, whatever I say, and don't you forget it," Brianna answered as she searched for her keys. "What's that noise?"

"It's just the TV. Are we done?" Damien's tone was impatient.

"It sounds like a woman screaming or something," Brianna said as she slipped on a shirt, tugging as it snagged her diamond earring.

"You tracking me, right? You know I haven't left the hotel. Where would I get a woman?"

"I'm not sure what you are capable of, but I do know I won't let you hurt anyone else if I can help it. Do me a favor and cut that damn TV off!"

"There, boss, it's off. See, it's quiet. Anything else?"

"Yeah, that's it," Brianna said. "I'll see you tomorrow night, and this will all be over. We never have to see or talk to each other again. Stay put in the room."

"Don't worry, I have enough things to do in the room to keep me occupied," Damien smirked as he hung up the phone.

Damien removed the pantyhose he had stuffed in Vanessa's mouth and slapped her face. Before she could scream, he stuck his burnt penis in her mouth to shut her up and held a knife to her throat. Vanessa gagged as he stuffed his penis deeper and deeper. She immediately became silent as tears rolled down her cheeks; she was tired. She felt degraded and defeated. Damien had done so much to her at that point that she knew she couldn't overpower him. The more she fought, the more violent he became.

Damien stood up and walked towards the bathroom, leaving Vanessa alone in the master suite. She quickly rolled to the front door. She thought if she could just get to the hallway, she could get help. She heard Damien running water in the bathtub. She lightly grabbed the doorknob and turned it, but it was locked. She would have to stand in order to open the door—it was her only chance.

Damien slowly went to the living room and saw Vanessa trying to escape. He panicked and grabbed Vanessa by her legs right before she turned the doorknob. He dragged her by her ankles back to the living room. Her attempt to escape had been a failure, and Damien was now ready to have some fun. He first cut off all her hair as she screamed through the pantyhose he forcefully stuffed back into her mouth. He sexually violated her with his fist. His penis was still sore from Brianna scolding it with the hot water, so he couldn't physically rape her. He brutally beat her to death and stuffed her inside her large Louis Vuitton luggage. That fast, Vanessa was gone as if she had never existed.

On the other side of town, Brianna hadn't liked the tone of Damien's voice. It was the same tone she had heard the day he violated her. Something just didn't feel right with Damien, and she couldn't let it go.

Brianna knew she didn't have time to stop by the hotel. She had more significant problems; she had to get to Craig before Dawn did something Brianna couldn't fix. She decided to call the front desk and have one of the male employees visit the penthouse suite. She hesitated because she knew Damien was dangerous, and anyone who interfered would possibly be killed. She made the call anyway.

Back at the hotel, Damien sat on the bed, exhausted from killing Vanessa. Just as Damien muscled up the strength to dispose of Vanessa's body, he got an unexpected knock. He glanced around the room. He had cleaned up well. The only blood was wrapped up in a blanket with Vanessa. Soon as he went to open the door, though, he noticed she had left a bloody fingerprint near the knob. He quickly ran to get a rag.

"One moment, please," he yelled from the bathroom.

"Sir, please open the door or I will have to use my key," the toothpick-of-a-receptionist warned from the other side of the door. "This is coming from the big boss. I'm sorry."

Damien opened the door and slid his arm into his jacket. "No need for that. I was just headed out. How can I help you?"

"We got a disturbance call from the room beneath you. Something about screams."

"Screams? Oh, I was watching a scary movie. The damn women always fall in the woods and scream. So predictable, huh?"

Damien glanced down the hallway, noticing another hotel staff member waiting at the elevator.

"Yes, those movies are horrible. This won't take long. Let me just look around, and then I can tell the boss everything is okay. Are you here alone?"

Damien put on his white-boy voice, the proper voice he used when he wanted to sound intelligent. "The hotel must pay you well. They have you doing security, too. I won't give you a hard time; you can look around. I have nothing to hide, and yes, I'm alone. Just please hurry—I have plans tonight."

"Thanks for cooperating. I'm sorry for disturbing you, sir. Everything seems to be good here. I hope this won't stop you from staying with us in the future. Our guest's safety is always a priority here. I hope you understand."

"It's fine. We all have jobs to do. Now I need to get to mines."

The man looked around, noticing Damien's personal belongings strewn about the room. "Nice luggage, my mom has one similar to that same one. They are pretty expensive. Are you checking out today?"

"Actually, I'm not checking out just yet. I'm just taking this luggage to my car. I plan on washing everything tomorrow. You guys should really have a laundry service here. It's a huge inconvenience."

"The hotel used to have one, and no one ever used it. They stopped offering that service last year. I'm sure that, since you are a special guest in the penthouse, they may make an exception."

"Thanks," Damien said, dragging Vanessa's body stuffed in her luggage toward the elevator, "I don't want to be a fuss. I guess it gives me something to do tomorrow. I'll just throw this in the trunk and get to my business meeting in the lobby."

He reached the elevator and pressed the down button. "Are you going down?" Damien impatiently asked.

"Yup, we are going down. You have yourself a great evening, sir."

The elevator dropped Damien off at the garage and the front desk receptionist called Brianna back and informed her there was nothing suspicious about Damien's room. He never mentioned the luggage.

Relieved, Brianna thanked the gentleman for checking.

She finally found her keys, which had fallen behind her bed, and without hesitation she rushed out the door. She ran to her car and peeled out.

She couldn't believe Craig would be stupid enough to visit Dawn alone. After all the things she had told him, he still thought he could reason with that animal.

As Brianna drove, she reminisced on all the fun times Craig and she had had as children. It brought tears to her eyes as she rushed to Dawn's apartment. Brianna made a vow that if Dawn hurt Craig, she would kill her on the spot, no more planning or fucking around. She would just have to go to jail, but no way would Dawn breathe another day after killing her brother. She figured the judge might take it easy on her after realizing she was the missing girl who had been tortured.

She arrived at Dawn's house and waited for the elevator. It took forever, so she ran over to the steps. Before she reached the doorknob, the door to the stairway opened. Detective Ross was standing behind Craig as he walked him out in handcuffs. Brianna instantly panicked, not knowing if Craig had killed Dawn and was being arrested for her murder. She wanted to say something to Craig but thought it would be wise to act as if she didn't know him. She couldn't blow her Bella cover, not when she was this close to ending it all.

Detective Ross quickly snapped her out of her thoughts.

"You sure are in a rush. Funny to run into you again. Bella, is it?"

"Yes, it's Bella. I'm late to a meeting with a client." She gave Craig a worried glance. Craig lowered his head as slow tears rolled down his cheeks.

"Oh, do you two know each other?" Detective Ross asked, noticing how they had looked at one another.

"You seem busy. I better get to that client's house before I get fired." Brianna weakly laughed.

"That client wouldn't happen to be Dawn, now would it?" Detective Ross asked, handing Craig off to his partner to walk him to the police car.

"I don't know anyone named Dawn, sir. I only have one client in this building, and that isn't her. Nice seeing you again." Brianna moved past the detective and started up the steps.

"Send Jerome my love when you see him. Also, if you could tell him, I'm now one hundred percent sure of the news I had to tell him." Detective Ross's voice faded as he left the stairwell and moved toward the apartment lobby.

Soon as he was out of sight, Brianna let out a long sigh. She was relieved Dawn hadn't killed Craig. She didn't know what had happened, but she knew her brother was alive, and for her that was enough. That detective was really starting to piss her off. If he reached Jerome before Brianna's plan could be revealed, he would screw up everything.

She sat on the staircase for about ten minutes, just crying. She had never wanted Craig to be involved in anything. That was the very reason she had waited so long to attack Dawn—so it could never come back on Craig.

Brianna pulled herself together, grabbed her Chanel bag, and threw on her Versace sunglasses. She stood tall and confident as she slowly left the staircase.

It was time to put everything to an end.

12
FAMILY DINNER

Dawn was annoyed she had to get ready for this stupid dinner party Papa had been planning. She had enjoyed the few days she'd had Papa to herself after leaving the hospital. She only made him leave so she could set Craig up. She hadn't been too thrilled about meeting Papa's new girlfriend, though. The thought of her Papa loving someone else made her sick to her stomach. She knew their relationship was serious because he took her to the hospital with him. Since Dawn had come home, all Papa had talked about was this Bella chick, and it was really starting to piss Dawn off. Not to mention Dr. Smidget had said she was gorgeous. Dawn felt an instant sense of envy.

Dawn took a long shower. When she stepped out of the shower, she glanced in the mirror. Her appearance was shocking. She looked terrible, and she felt unattractive. Her hair was still shaved, and only peach fuzz had grown back.

She threw on her wig. As she tightened the wig, she noticed the scar from the bullet that had entered her head. A boiling rage overtook her, and she ground her teeth as she imagined how she would get back at Brianna.

She sat on the bed with her white towel wrapped around her naked, frail body, and she thought of ways to find Brianna. The problem was, Brianna was still technically missing, so the internet was no help to Dawn. She searched high and low and came up with nothing except missing articles. Dawn found herself laughing at the picture of Brianna from the "*Have You Seen Me*" article, which predicted how she would look as an adult. Their image of Brianna was totally off. Her features had changed drastically, and she was much prettier than they had predicted. She finally gave up searching the internet and began to look for something to wear.

Dawn felt off. She couldn't quite put her finger on it, but she knew the feeling had started after Craig left with Detective Ross. What was it trying to tell her? She decided to call Papa to distract her.

"Hey, Papa," Dawn said as she searched her closet for another outfit. "It's your favorite girl."

"Hey, baby girl. I'm so happy you called. You're on your way, right?" Papa sounded excited.

Dawn pulled out an outfit, but she had slimmed down and it no longer fit, so she returned it. "Not yet, but I'm getting dressed. I just wanted to hear your voice. Do you need me to bring anything?"

"Just bring your pretty self. Bella has really gone all out for this dinner. She got all the food catered, and between you and me, that was a blessing. That woman has many qualities, but cooking is not one of them." Papa laughed.

"Papa, I called to talk to you, not to hear about your girlfriend. I seriously need a drink."

"We have everything, even your favorite wine, Chardonnay. You know I don't drink anymore, so it will just be the ladies sipping tonight. Dawn, can you do me a favor?"

"Sure. What do you need, Papa?"

"Please try to give Bella a chance. I know this is hard for you, especially after hearing what happened to your mother. No one will ever be Sandy, but just try for me, please."

Dawn snorted. "What do you mean, what happened to my mother? Her being selfish and just living her own life? Papa, I'm grown, and I'm tired of chasing behind Mama."

"No, Dawn. It's something else. I'll tell you at dinner. Hurry up and get here. I've missed you so much!"

"Papa, you just left my house yesterday," she laughed.

Dawn hung up the phone and finally decided to wear an all-black Gucci pantsuit Craig had bought her a few years ago. It fit her well enough because she had still been pretty slim at the time he bought it. She had only gained weight from the pregnancy, which she drastically lost in the hospital while fighting for her life.

Dawn dabbed on some lipstick, grabbed her keys, and opened the door. Suddenly she was filled with a premonition that she shouldn't leave the house. Ignoring this feeling, she composed herself and walked out the front door.

For some reason, she looked at her apartment before shutting and locking the door. She didn't know why she looked at her place as if it would be her last time there.

She arrived at Papa's house fifteen minutes early. It was just her and Papa, and she was thrilled to be alone with him.

Papa hugged her, then handed her a bottle of wine. "Here, baby. Bella got you this wine. She left a note asking us to get the party started without her. She is running a little behind. But the food will be here on time."

"Thank God. I need a drink. Oh, she has taste, I see. Louis Jadot Chardonnay. This place is really nice, too." She laughed. "Who are you dating, Papa, a celebrity?"

"Not a celebrity, but she does come from money. I'm glad you like the wine." He cleared his throat. "I'm also glad we are alone, so we can talk about Mama."

"Do we have to?" Dawn asked as she poured herself a glass of Chardonnay, swirling the wine and sniffing it before taking a sip. "Can't we just enjoy the moment? Why don't you tell me what's been going on with you?"

"Dawn, she's dead!" Papa blurted out.

"What? Dead? She can't be!" Dawn tensed up in disbelief.

"She is. I'm sorry to tell you this way, but you wouldn't let me get it out. She was on the news. Her body was found in the Detroit River."

Tears welled in Dawn's eyes. "Oh my God. Poor Mama. She must've been so scared. Did she commit suicide? What happened?"

"According to the news, she was murdered. I don't have many details. Tomorrow I'm going to the police station to meet with Detective Ross. He had something else to talk to me about, but I'll be sure to grill him about Mama's death."

Now the tears were pouring down Dawn's cheeks. "This is a child's worst nightmare. Why is all this happening?"

Papa took Dawn in his arms and rocked her. "I don't know, baby. I just don't know. Have you talked to your brother?"

"No. But I know Damien is devastated. He loved Mama the most, even more than he loved either one of us."

"I know this is hard, but we'll get through it together. I loved your mother, too. She was my first love, and although we didn't reconnect after I was released, I never wanted anything to happen to her. I actually feel bad, like it's my fault."

"How could it possibly be your fault?"

"Because I thought she didn't want anything to do with me, so I was angry with her. When I got out of prison and she was nowhere to be found, I resented her—when all along, she was dead. I didn't even go looking for her." Tears spilled from Papa's eyes. "That woman loved me to death, and I let her down."

"It's not your fault. Mama knew you loved her. She would want us to be strong, so let's toughen up.

We will get through this dinner and bury Mama when that time comes. I guess her leaving Damien and me will make this process easier in a way. We haven't seen her in years."

"You're right. Let's just get through dinner. One thing at a time."

Papa roughly wiped his eyes and sat back in his seat. Just as he sat down, the doorbell rang as the caterers arrived with the food. They arranged the dishes on the table, with baskets of breadsticks in the middle. Dawn wasted no time grabbing one, along with some butter. The caterers quickly left.

"This expensive wine is no joke. I feel nice already. Actually, I feel stuck, like I can't move. I probably shouldn't be drinking with the meds Dr. Smidget gave me, but the hell with it." Dawn took another swallow of wine.

"Do you think that's smart to drink on prescription drugs?" Papa asked with a concerned look on his face.

"Do you think I care? I need it, but I must admit I feel super weird, like I'm moving in slow motion." Dawn grabbed the bottle.

"Ok, you little lightweight," Papa said with a laugh. "Don't be drunk early. You know your father was a drinking champ; you can't be all sloppy after a few glasses of wine. Didn't I teach anything?"

"Papa, I'm only on my third glass. Let me live. After the news I just heard, I'm surprised this whole bottle isn't gone. Where is your girlfriend? I'm hungry!" Dawn slammed the bottle down on the table.

Papa grabbed the bottle. "I think you've had enough."

"Papa, put that bottle down!" Dawn yelled, and Papa released the bottle. She continued to drink. About fifteen minutes later, the front door opened.

"Hey, baby!" Brianna yelled from the hallway, which was partially blocked off from the dining area. "I'm so sorry I'm late."

"It's cool. Dawn and I needed some alone time anyway. But now we are starving! Hurry up!" Papa slapped another breadstick in his mouth.

"Hi, Dawn," Brianna said, smiling broadly as she sat opposite Dawn. "Nice to meet you."

"Don't be rude, Dawn," Papa said, noticing the way Dawn was frowning at Brianna. "Say hello back."

"What the fuck is she doing here?" Dawn asked as she tried to get up.

"Oh, don't even try to move," Brianna said with a dismissive wave of her hand. "You are paralyzed from the waist down. So let's eat!" She removed the metal lid from her plate.

"What do you mean she's paralyzed?" Papa asked, confused. "She is recovering from getting shot, but she's not paralyzed. Do you two know each other or something?"

"Maybe you should tell him how we know each other, Dawn," Brianna said as she slammed a gun on the table.

"What the fuck, Bella?" Papa's eyebrows raised, his voice strengthened as he pushed back his chair. "Put that damn gun up. What the hell is going on?"

"Tell him, Dawn. You are mighty quiet tonight. Did that wine get to you?" Brianna smirked as she picked up her dinner knife and began cutting her steak.

"Papa, she's crazy!" Dawn exclaimed. "She's the one who shot me! Kill her, Papa, before she kills me!"

"You're hard to die, I'll give you that," Brianna said. "When I shot you, that was my second attempt to kill you. The first time I tried to kill you was at Craig and I's family cabin. Oh, you look so confused. Craig is my adopted brother, and that ski trip you all took was at my family's house."

"What do you mean, Craig is your brother?"

Brianna ignored Dawn's question and she roughly stuck the fork in her vegetables. "Anyway, I was there too. I hid in the closet in my father's office. I tried to poison you, but you only took two sips of your coffee. Unfortunately, it wasn't enough to take you out."

"Bella, what the hell are you talking about? You tried to kill my daughter? Twice?" Papa rose, ready to launch himself at Brianna.

Brianna picked up the gun and aimed it at Papa. "Sit the fuck down before you meet my friend Mr. Bullet. Don't think because you have some good dick, I won't lay your ass down. I'll let you rest next to your deceitful-ass daughter."

A look of genuine fear entered Papa's eyes. "Look, calm down. I'm just trying to figure out what the hell is going on."

"What's going on, Jerome, is your daughter choked me out on the street, dragged me into a dead man's house, left me for dead, and a few days later set me on fire. That's what the fuck is going on."

"Papa, don't listen to her," Dawn pleaded, still paralyzed. "She's clearly deranged."

"Deranged? Jerome, it's time you know the real truth. I'm Brianna! I'm the missing girl your daughter tortured and your son raped. Damien took my virginity, and Dawn was so upset that she couldn't control me that she tried to kill me. Now *that's* the truth!"

"Wait, Bella. Are you telling me you are Brianna?

The little girl Dawn used to play with? This is too much. Dawn, what is everyone talking about? Tell me something, baby girl." It broke his heart, discovering who Dawn really was.

"Papa, they are all fucking liars!" Dawn yelled.

Brianna pinned Dawn's hand to the table with a cake knife. "Bitch, confess. Tell him right now!"

Dawn screamed in pain. "Papa, stop this crazy bitch! Help me!"

"Bella," Papa said, "I can't sit here and watch you hurt my daughter. You're just gonna have to shoot me."

"Fine," Brianna bluntly answered as she shot Papa in the arm.

"Shit! You shot me! Bella, you fucking shot me!"

"Listen the fuck up. I'm not playing with you crazy motherfuckers. I don't want to hurt you, Jerome. I promise you, I don't. I love you. But no one, I mean no one, will stop me from killing this bitch. As a matter of fact, let's bring Damien to the party. He's part of the family, right?" Brianna picked up her phone and called Damien.

"He's not a part of this family!" Papa screamed as he grabbed a handkerchief off the table and tied it around his bloody arm.

Brianna watched Dawn like a hulk as she spoke into the phone. "Damien, good boy answering on the first ring. It's time!"

"T-t-t-time time for what?" Dawn stuttered. It hit Dawn at that moment why she had felt off earlier that day. It was the feeling of something bad about to happen. It was the feeling of death. She had felt it before, but this time it was stronger. She realized she might never see her apartment again.

"I should've known Damien was behind this shit!" Papa cried. "That's exactly why I hate that little bastard! So, Bella, that was you who mysteriously called me at the hospital? That was you who said Dawn strangled you?"

"Be patient. All in due time. I did try to warn you, but you didn't even investigate. Even after Sheryl tried to tell you, you still didn't do shit. You think your precious daughter is an angel. She killed your best friend Ralph, too, but he was a piece of crap anyway."

Papa just sat there, his mouth open in disbelief.

"Dawn," Brianna continued, "I noticed you were stuttering. Are you okay, bestie?"

"Fuck you!" Dawn tried to yell, drool running from the corner of her mouth, but only faint sounds came out.

"Well, your Papa fucks me pretty well. Tell her, Jerome." Brianna laughed.

"I won't be fucking you no more, I tell you that shit."

"That's sad, Jerome. We had such a great sex life.

The best sexual chemistry I've ever had with a man."
Brianna leaned across the table toward Dawn.
"Dawn, it always annoyed me how you would clean
your ear with your pinky finger."

"Whhhat? What did you sayyyyy?" Dawn
stuttered. Her mind was foggy. She felt weaker by the
minute, and she knew whatever Brianna had put in
the wine was starting to take her senses. She couldn't
smell, her hearing was fading, and she could barely
see.

"Uh-oh, the baby has a stuttering problem. I know
you are starting to feel weird. See, the first time I
tried to kill you, I didn't know the correct dosage to
poison someone slowly. This time I had the dosage
perfectly. I kept you alive long enough for you to tell
the truth, but fast enough to die."

Brianna picked up a second knife and chopped off
Dawn's pinky from the hand pinned to the table.

Dawn screamed, trying to thrash but unable to
move. "What the fuck did you do that for? I swear if
I could move, I would rip your fucking head off!
Papa, why are you just sitting there? Help me!"

The pain gave her the ability to speak normally for
a moment. She tried to tell her mind to snap back.
She felt she was slowly losing herself; she couldn't
smell at all, and her vision was blurred.

"You couldn't rip my head off, bitch, if I handed

it to you," Brianna answered. "Your organs are failing, and you should be losing your sight by now. Just hang in there long enough for Damien to get here."

"Bella, please stop," Papa pleaded as he tried to stop the bleeding in his arm. "If you ever really loved me, please stop."

"Okay, Jerome. I'll stop torturing her—if she tells you the truth about everything."

Brianna took a lighter and burned the tip of Dawn's pinky finger to stop the bleeding. Dawn screamed like a cow being butchered.

"See, I can be nice," Brianna said. "I stopped her bleeding. Now talk." She pointed the gun at Dawn.

"Okay, shit. Here's the fucking truth. I am everything Brianna said I was. I'm a maniac. I'm a fucking psychopath. I think different from the average mind, and pretending has been the hardest-t-t-t part. Pretending to actually love, I can't lov-v-ve. I'm incapable of love. I don't think I even love *you*, Papa."

Dawn's words made sense in her own mind, but aloud they were scattered and shaky.

"Don't say that," Papa answered. "It's not true. Don't let this break you. The hell with Bella. Stay strong!"

Dawn searched the room for a weapon before she

completely lost her sight. Even if she found something, though, her legs wouldn't move. She tried multiple times, but she was stuck in the chair, unable to move anything but her head.

"Are you listening, Papa?" she said. "I am truly evil. I am your worst nightmare, literally. I tortured you in your sleep for years. I don't love you, and when Brianna just shot you, I actually smirked. I think we all deserve pain, and I love inflicting it."

"So what Sheryl said about you is true? Were your tears for your mother fake, too?"

"Fuck Sheryl! I should've killed that stinky pile of nothing a long time ago. She's worthless. As for Mama, my beautiful, perfectly-shaped mother…the one who provided oxygen in my lungs as she carried me in her womb…" She trailed off, lost in memory.

After a few moments, she went on. "Mama always smelled good and made the best biscuits in the world. It was Mama who ran my hot bath water with the bubbles. It was Mama who washed my hair and took such pride in keeping it healthy and long. It was Mama who cried when I was sick. Good ole Momma."

Dawn smiled at Papa. At that moment, Damien quietly walked in and stood in the doorway where only Brianna could see him, listening.

"Dawn, stop fucking around!" Papa yelled. "What happened to your mother?" Papa wanted to hate her after what she'd said, but he couldn't. She was still his precious Dawn, even after all the terror she'd caused.

Dawn's speech was changing drastically. Although she said a lot, it was difficult to make sense of much of it.

"See, Mama had a problem keeping her big mouth shut," she went on, blinking her eyes rapidly. "It's Brianna's fault Mama is dead."

Dawn noticed that the more she blinked, the less blurry everyone was. It was only a temporary way to keep her sight, but she refused to just sit there and go blind. Deep inside, she was panicking. She knew her time was coming to an end, but she would never bow down. She had woken up that morning feeling off, and now she knew why. Her spirit was very much alive, but her poor body was tired. She was literally a dead woman talking.

Damien calmly listened and tried to make out as much as he could from Dawn's fumbling attempts to communicate.

"How the fuck is it my fault?" Brianna finally demanded.

"Mama saw me come out of Ralph's house that night, the night I tried to burn your ass up, and she wouldn't leave it alone," Dawn replied. "Mama threatened to turn me in one day, so I scared the shit out of her. That's why she left Sheryl's house. But then, when my life was going pretty good, she showed up talking about telling Detective Ross. I took her to dinner that night and strangled her in an alley. I put her dead body in the trunk of my c-c-a-a-a-r-r-r-r and threw her in the river-r-r-r."

As Dawn's stutter worsened, she leaned her head back as if ready to die. She still had some fight left in her, though. She quickly lifted her head back up and tried to focus her eyes on Brianna.

"You did *what* to my mother?" Damien screamed. "You crazy fucking bitch! What's wrong with you?"

Damien ran to the table and stabbed Dawn with the same knife he killed Vanessa with the day before. He slowly pulled the knife out and stabbed her again. Papa stood up to help Dawn but froze as he noticed she was smiling. It was the first time Papa had seen the evil in Dawn's face, and he decided not to help her. As much as he loved Dawn, he realized at that very moment she had a rotten soul. A soul that couldn't be repaired.

"Damien, sit down! That's enough!" Brianna yelled. "This is my show, and you are just my guest. We will sit at this table as a family and eat dinner. Now Dawn, what the hell did you do to get Craig arrested?"

"Fuck Craig's booty-eating ass." She murmured with blood coming from her mouth. Damien had stabbed her twice in the chest, barely missing her heart. "I got him arrested for my attempted murder. You will never see him again."

Dawn turned her head toward Papa. "Papa, I can't see anymore. My chest is burning. Please help me."

Papa ignored her pleas for help. "Did you hurt my brother Robby, too? Are you the reason he stopped speaking?" He was finally disgusted with Dawn, and he couldn't pretend she was anything but what she really was: evil incarnate.

"Yes. But forget Uncle Robby right now, Papa. Y'all are asking too many questions. I'm bleeding, and I'm slowly losing my ability to hear. I can't hear! I can't see! Papa, help!"

"You just lied on Craig and had him arrested for nothing," Brianna said. "You haven't changed at all. You don't deserve mercy."

Dawn decided to try being nice. "Brianna, I'm sorry I tried to kill you. I'm sorry I got Craig arrested for my shooting. Damien caused all of this. Why are you just after m-m-me?"

"I've dealt with Damien. It's your turn. I'm waiting for you to take your last breath so I can finally live again. Actually, let's speed up the process."

Brianna shot Dawn twice, first in one leg and then in the other. Dawn barely flinched. She had already lost all feeling in her lower body.

Damien moved toward Brianna, his eyes on the gun. "Can I shoot her? She tortured me and killed my mother. I went to jail for all her murders. She gave me nightmares and made my life hell. She took my man and my life. I deserve to kill her. I want to be the one. She possessed me and made me do horrible things. I'm a victim, too."

"First, prove you want her dead," Brianna said as she tapped the bottom of the gun on the table.

Damien stood up, carved two deep slices on Dawn's face with a knife and then used a pizza roller to smash the side of Dawn's head. Dawn screamed feebly.

Papa lowered his head. It was too much to watch.

"Pick up your head and watch!" Brianna shouted at him.

Tears filled Papa's eyes as he looked up. "I thought you drugged her. Just let her be. Why do you have to torture her?"

Papa felt like he was in a nightmare that he desperately wanted to end. He wanted to stop everyone from hurting his baby girl, but he loved Sandy. He couldn't believe Dawn had killed her own mother. His thoughts were confused, and all he could do was hope everything would be over soon.

"Let her be?" Dawn asked, blood running down her face. "Papa, you think I deserve this? You think I deserve to die? I never hurt you, did I, Papa?"

"Shut up!" Brianna demanded. "Everyone shut up! Damien, sit back down."

They sat in silence for a few minutes. Dawn's eyes rolled to the back of her head and her body relaxed as she finally gave up the fight.

Damien was nearly jumping with excitement. "Can I shoot her now? I will just shoot her one time in the arm. Please give me something for my mother's revenge. Please, can I?"

"One shot and give me the gun back. Don't forget I have that chip inside you. If anything happens to me, my friend has specific instructions to hit the button, and boom, you are gone."

Papa shook his head to warn Brianna, but it was too late. She handed the gun to Damien, and the energy in the room shifted immediately. Everything slowed down. The room had a chill, and everything moved in slow motion. It felt like something from a movie.

Brianna quickly realized giving Damien the gun had been a huge mistake. She had allowed her need for revenge on Dawn to clutter her mind. She had figured Damien killing Dawn would bring great pleasure, and she wouldn't have to be a murderer. She had never wanted to be a murderer. If Damien killed Dawn, then it wouldn't have to be on Brianna's conscience.

The sound of the first gunshot was deafening in the confines of the room. Dawn's limp body fell to the floor, a hole in her forehead. Blood and brain fat were splattered all over the table.

Brianna looked into Damien's red eyes, and she saw pure evil. Fear and regret took over her body. She reflected over her life and knew she would never see her parents again. She knew she had fucked up. She knew she had given her life to Damien on a silver platter.

Damien pulled Dawn's chair that she no longer sat in toward Papa and sat in front of him. "Hey, Daddy! Can I call you Daddy? I always hated that Papa shit anyway. You look worried, Daddy. You should be."

"Okay, Damien," Brianna said, trying to keep the panic out of her voice. "Give me back the gun!"

"Bitch, you are dumber than I thought. First, you thought I would believe you put a bomb inside me. Then, you actually gave me a loaded gun. You really thought you owned me, huh? Now you sit your dumb ass down. Go ahead, sit next to your man." Damien laughed as he swung the gun around.

"There *is* a chip inside you!"

In answer, Damien ripped off his shirt and showed her an open wound where he had removed her horrible stitch job. Brianna's legs started to shake as she walked over to sit next to Papa, as Damien had instructed.

Papa lowered his eyes to Dawn's body sprawled on the floor, then quickly looked up again. "Damien, leave her out of this. I'm still your father. I love you, Damien."

"Love me? You never fucking loved me! You never cared! You just loved Dawn and look at the piece of shit she turned out to be. Look at her! Look at your precious Dawn!"

"I did love you. I just, I just, I wanted you to be a man. Shit, I didn't even have a father." Papa reached for Brianna's hand.

"I don't want to hear your sad story. How cute, you two holding hands in y'all last moments. You love her, huh? Brianna is pretty now—oh I forgot, Bella. She wasn't always this pretty. Did she tell you I fucked her?"

"More like raped me," Brianna mumbled under her breath.

"I'm sorry, did you say something? It doesn't matter now, cause Daddy, we both fucked her. I have to admit, you look just as young as me. Who would have ever known we would fuck the same bitch?" Damien laughed.

"Bella, you were sleeping with Damien?" Papa asked in a hurt tone. "Damien, I thought you were..." He paused.

"Thought what? I was gay? Go ahead and say it."

"Baby, he's talking about when I went missing as a kid," Brianna whispered to Papa. "He took my virginity. I never cheated on you, and I loved you more than any man I've ever met. I just wanted to be free from Dawn. I hope you can forgive me for all I've done to protect myself from your kids." She didn't want him to die thinking she had cheated on him, but she also wanted him to know his children had tortured her.

"Bella, Brianna, or whoever the fuck you want to be, did I tell you to talk?" Damien slapped her in the temple with the gun as she had done to him days prior.

"Hold the fuck up now, Damien," Papa protested. "You didn't have to do that to her." He leaned down to help Brianna up, but she was on the side of his injured arm, and he didn't have the strength to pick her up off the floor.

"Don't tell me shit. Actually, this conversation is getting pretty boring, and you know better than anyone how I hate to be bored. Thanks for giving me life, and thanks for ruining my life. Would you be a good daddy for once in your life and do me a favor?"

Damien rose and aimed the gun at the center of Papa's head.

"Wait, Damien," Papa pleaded. "We can talk. You will have no family if you kill me—I'm all you have left."

"Tell Mama I said hello!" Damien coldly stated.

"Damien, no! Don't do this!" Papa covered his face with his hands.

Damien pulled the trigger for the second time, hitting Papa in the middle of his forehead. He died instantly.

Brianna screamed. She rushed to Papa and held his lifeless body in her arms.

"I'm so sorry, Jerome," she whispered into his ear. "I'm so sorry. I never wanted you to get hurt. I love you. Baby, I love you so much. That part was always real."

She saw Jerome's blood spreading across her white Armani suit, and her hands began to shake uncontrollably. "You fucking maniac! You killed him, you killed him. I hate you. You pathetic, insecure, jealous, evil, manipulative piece of shit. You are nothing! A fucking disgrace. I hate you!"

Brianna screamed to Damien as tears rushed down her face. She was so hurt and numb. As she grieved, her sadness rapidly turned into rage.

"Aww, isn't this so cute? You really did love my

father. This is truly adorable. How many bullets do you think are left in this gun? Oh, you don't have to answer, I'll just show you. Now you sit the fuck down!"

"I will not sit down! Kill me standing. I will never bow down to you or Dawn again, fuck you—"

Brianna stopped speaking as she felt a burning sensation in her right arm. Damien had shot her!

Damien moved toward her. "Now I shot you in the arm, just as you did to my father. Stand your pretty ass up! Stand up in your two-thousand-dollar red-bottom stilettos that you will never wear again." He sat on the end of the table.

"You don't scare me, and you are out of bullets, dumb ass!" Brianna grabbed a knife and swung it at Damien's face, but missed.

"You are one stupid bitch. You could've started a new life, and no one would have ever known you were alive, but nope! You wanted to be a Boss Bitch! You wanted to own motherfuckers and shit. Didn't you?"

Damien slapped Brianna down to the floor and snatched the knife out of her hand.

"And you feel tough?" Brianna said, taunting him. "You feel like a man standing over me as I lay here wounded? You are a coward and a disgrace. Your father hated your guts, Dawn couldn't stand you, and Craig pitied you. Your own mother ran away from you. Look around: You've killed everyone, and you still won't be happy."

"Maybe I'll never be happy, but I don't need happiness. I have me. I have Damien. Now maybe I should burn your pubic hair, since you have so much to say."

Damien ripped off Brianna's white pants. She lay there exposed for a moment before she stood up to run. She ran as fast as she could toward the front door, Damien in pursuit.

Brianna took a split second to picture her mother's face, and she smiled. She thought of Craig pulling her from Ralph's burning house, and a tear rolled down her cheek. She laughed at how scared Craig had been to ask his adoptive parents if this strange beat-up girl could come live with them. She thought of her pink room and all the fun she'd had with her real parents before she went missing. She then thought of all the things Damien and Dawn had done to her. She replayed Craig's voicemail in her mind:

"We have to call this thing off with Damien. He's not who I thought he was. I can't explain over the phone, just please trust me. We have to let it go. I'm on my way to fix things with Dawn. Bella, we can finally move forward. Let's just move away or something. I love you."

A tear rolled down her cheek as she imagined how different things could have been if she had just listened to Craig. It saddened her to think she would never see her parents again.

Without a second thought, she grabbed her spare gun from the drawer near the front door. She switched off the safety and lifted the gun. *Pop!* The gunshot echoed as if the space was empty. The room was still and quiet.

The gunshot exploded in her ears. She fell to the floor in slow motion. She sat in her bodily fluids as her body shook, as if from a seizure. She coughed blood from her mouth and turned to face Papa. Her eyes got bigger and bigger. Then her body faded as she sat there with a blank stare. She died looking at Papa; he was the last thing she saw.

Damien walked over, sat on top of Brianna's lifeless body and whispered. "It's always one in the chamber, you stupid Bitch!"

He turned her face so her deceased eyes could look at him. Although she was dead, Damien stabbed her corpse repeatedly. He then roughly spread her legs open and stuck his penis in her anus. After three strokes, he laughed, grabbed one of the dinner candles from the table, and set Brianna's vagina on fire. Brianna had been helplessly beaten. She may have won the fight against Dawn, but she had lost the war to Damien.

Damien sat back in his original seat and removed the silver lid from the dinner plate. It was lobster drizzled in a butter sauce, fresh asparagus, a well-done steak, and a baked potato.

Using a table napkin, Damien wiped Brianna's blood off the knife and then used the knife to cut his steak. He neatly ate the entire meal as pools of blood spread from the corpses of Dawn, Papa, and Brianna.

Damien stood up and flipped Dawn's body on her back. He fixed her crooked wig and gently touched her hand. Her hand wasn't cold, but it wasn't warm anymore. He put all her fingers together. He got up from the floor and grabbed a bowl filled with hot water and soap. He washed Dawn's face and neck. He grabbed some band-aids from behind the bathroom mirror. He snatched the plush gray sheets off Brianna's bed. He covered Dawn's entire body with the sheet except for her face. He put two band-aids on the cuts he had given her. He lay next to her and thought of all their memories growing up.

"Who owns who now?" he mumbled. He placed the knife on his chest as if it was a newborn baby. It wasn't long before he blacked out.

13

DAMIEN'S SECRET

"Damien, wake up!" Dr. Smidget yelled, shaking my body. "You had another one of those blackouts."

Dr. Smidget helped me up from the floor.

"Who are you?" I asked, holding my head and looking around. "Where am I?"

"I'm Doctor Smidget. I'm your doctor here at Lakewood Mental Institution. You were out for quite a while—I'm afraid you may have had another episode. Your roommate came to tell us. How are you feeling?"

"Why would I be at a mental institution? The last thing I remember was looking at my dead sister." I lowered my head, remembering how I had killed Dawn.

"Craig, I need your help over here," Dr. Smidget

called out.

I looked around the all-white mental institution and spotted Craig. "Oh, good, there you are. Finally, someone familiar. I thought you were arrested? Everything is a blur. Can we go?" I asked Craig as I looked around to gather my things.

"Am I Brandon or Craig today, Damien?" Craig answered nonchalantly. "Come on, let's get you up on the bed."

"Craig, stop playing. I don't want to get on the bed; I want to leave. I'm sorry about Brianna. I'll tell you all about it when we're alone. I had no choice, Craig—it was her or me." I raised my eyebrows as I noticed his outfit. "Why are you dressed like that?"

Dr. Smidget cleared his throat. "Damien, Craig works here, and you don't know him personally. Please lie down; I don't want to have to call the other nurses to restrain you."

"I *do* know him. He's Mr. Ralph's son Brandon, but he was later adopted as Craig. My sister Dawn was going to marry him, but she got him arrested. It's a long story, but he's my lover, and I'm ready to go. Come on, Craig." I reached out for Craig's arm.

"Mr. Ralph didn't have any kids. You know that. In one of our sessions, you told me that Mr. Ralph constantly told you he didn't have a son. You imagined a boy named Brandon, and you later changed his name to Craig. Every time a new male nurse works here, they become your imaginary Brandon. I know you may be confused, but I need you on the bed."

"You are a damn liar! He is Craig, and I fucked him. I fucked him in the cabin, and I fucked him in the snow!" My voice rose to a scream. "Tell them, Craig, tell them how we made love. Come on, baby, I'm ready to come out now. I'm sorry for keeping us a secret for so long. Help me get out of here, and we can fix everything."

"Enough, Damien!" Dr. Smidget barked. "Craig is married with two kids, and you don't know him outside this mental institution. Stop it!"

"You all are crazy! I need Dawn. Did I miss her funeral? Brianna made me kill her. Can you believe it, Craig? How did I get here? Can I make a phone call?"

"What funeral?" Dr. Smidget answered. "Your twin sister died at birth, and you pretend to be her. When you become Dawn, you fade in and out of reality. You live in this make-believe world in your mind for a few weeks before you come back to reality. It's your way of escaping the truth. Now I need you to calm down."

Dr. Smidget moved closer, revealing the needle in his hand.

"The truth?" I replied. "What is the truth? You are wrong. Dawn didn't die at birth. Dawn has been with me our entire life. Are you nuts? She was just here—remember, Craig?" Tears welled up in my eyes. "I threw her off the mountain, and she had amnesia. Remember Brianna shot her twice, remember?"

Craig looked unmoved, completely ignoring Damien. He turned to look at Dr. Smidget as if he was waiting for confirmation to call for help.

"Do you really think you could throw someone off a mountain, and they would survive?" Dr. Smidget said. "Think about it, Damien. Brianna couldn't have shot Dawn because Brianna died in the fire when you burned her alive. I hate to tell you this, but Dawn died at birth. She doesn't exist, and you killed Brianna years ago."

"She does exist. I saw Mama talking to her all the time. Dawn and Brianna were best friends, and Dawn was Papa's favorite. Brianna started dating Papa just to get close to Dawn to kill her." I turned toward Craig. "I made you date Dawn because she started acting suspiciously. Remember?"

Craig said nothing as he readied the restraints.

"I'm sorry, Damien—I've never met any of these people," he finally confessed. "But let me help you get settled. We know you hate needles, but it will relax you."

"No!" I cried. "So I killed my mother? Was it me? I did all those horrible things? I loved Mama. How could I?" I wept.

"Yes, Damien," Dr. Smidget said patiently. "We go over this every few weeks. I'm so sorry, but you killed your mother, you killed Mr. Ralph, you killed Brianna and your Aunt Sheryl. Again, Dawn died at birth. You've been here at the institution since you were sixteen years old; you are now twenty-three. You were found by Detective Ross when you murdered your mother and your Aunt Sheryl. You stayed in the house with their corpses for three months, which is why the courts declared you insane."

"No! You are a liar. Dawn did it. I saw her. You all saw her! Craig, you were going to marry her, and you got her pregnant. I can't believe you don't remember. What about your sister Bella? Tell Dr. Smidget Brianna isn't dead. Tell him she's Bella."

Dr. Smidget sighed. "Craig, call for backup. This isn't going anywhere."

"What about Papa? Didn't he whip my ass? Didn't he put me in the hospital?"

"No, Damien, but he did come here to see you when he was released from prison. You were declared insane at your trial, and all your father's charges were dropped. I hate to tell you this, but you had an episode when your father left, and one of the patients named Mike physically attacked you, and we had to strain you both for three days."

"Doctor, who do you think you are talking to?" I asked, frustrated. "You think I'm some type of fucking looney. Do you think I let some nutjob in here kick my ass? Who is Mike? Where is he now?"

Dr. Smidget began reviewing his chart. "Calm down, Damien. I would hate to sedate you after an episode. I'm trying to do this the easy way. We don't want you to have a long blackout again—it's dangerous."

Emma approached the room, flanked by two nurses.

"Mrs. Emma!" I cried. "Please help me! Tell them you were the counselor at the prison. Tell them I was there. She knows me; she will tell you!"

"Hi, Damien," Emma said calmly as she entered the room. "I'm glad to see you are coming around. I am your therapist here at the facility. I know that after one of these episodes, you get extremely stressed and overwhelmed. Things probably feel confusing, but Dr. Smidget has your best interests in mind. We can have a one-on-one tomorrow, okay? Right now, I need you to comply."

"Not okay, bitch! Tell them! Oh, I see; everyone in here wants to make me look crazy. Put all the players in one room, and I'm the psycho. Is that how this works? What about jail? I went to jail, and there was a man there named Crazy Joe. He was my cellmate, and you were my counselor. I don't know why you are lying, Emma, but this ain't right!"

I backed into the corner of the room, raising my hands to defend myself.

"Crazy Joe is your roommate here at the facility, Damien," Dr. Smidget explained, shaking his head. "We asked you to stop calling him Crazy Joe because it's offensive to the other patients, remember?"

"So, am I even gay?" I asked as I looked around. Suddenly the mental institution started looking very familiar. My heart slowed down, and I realized someone had stuck me with the needle while I was distracted.

"We can't say for sure," Emma answered. "You are usually pretty obsessed with the male nurses, but from what we know, you've only had sex once, and it was with Brianna before you killed her. I have to give you the facts, as harsh as they sound, so you know who you truly are. This is the only way you can start to heal."

"You're saying I made all this up so I wouldn't have to face the truth? The nightmares, too?" I shook, thinking of Mama.

"Yes, Damien, the nightmares too," Dr. Smidget answered. "Lie down now, and if you are settled when you awake, we will let you go back to your regular room."

"Okay, I will cooperate. Just answer this. Everything I blamed Dawn for—I'm the one who actually did it? Up until the age of sixteen, right?"

"Yes, and it seems you've always kept Dawn as an imaginary sister since you were really young," Emma admitted.

"So, what changed at sixteen? Please tell me."

"Damien, at sixteen, you threw your Aunt Sheryl down the stairs and broke her neck after she found your mother's body in the basement. The guilt from murdering your mother is what made you officially insane. Everything from that moment forward was all made up in your mind. The truth is, you lived alone for three months with both of their deceased bodies until Detective Ross found you and arrested you for the other murders. You were then sent here, and you haven't left since."

"But it felt so real. I saw Dawn do those things."

"We all play a character in your mind, Damien, whatever character makes you feel like the victim. It's the way you deal with guilt. Sometimes I'm Dawn's doctor. Sometimes Craig is your lover. Sometimes Joe is your cellmate, or maybe Emma is your prison counselor. Sometimes you bring Brianna back to life and change her name to something else – Bella, for instance – so you don't have to face what you did to her. In your mind, you make us who you want us to be to hide your secret—your *true* secret."

"What's my true secret?" I asked as my eyes filled with tears.

"Your true secret that you keep from yourself is that you are a cold-blooded serial killer," Emma answered. "Everyone knows, but you hide it from yourself."

My eyes drooped as the tranquilizer took hold.

"Get some rest," Emma added. "That's enough for today. We will talk more tomorrow."

I woke up in a familiar place. It was my home. It had four white walls and a roommate who yelled all day. I probably deserved much worse. I probably deserved not to be there at all.

I felt weak from the drugs Dr. Smidget had given me the day before. Some things I remembered, and some I didn't. According to the staff there, I chose what I wanted to remember. Aren't we lucky we have choices in life? I often chose not to be normal. I could've pretended to be a good son. I could've lived my life like the rest of the boring assholes. I chose to live outside reality, though.

Sometimes, I really messed up. Killing Mama was a fuck up moment. I really did love her. She just wouldn't shut up that day! Apparently, she saw me leave Mr. Ralph's the night I started the fire, and she wouldn't let it go. She was in the basement washing, and I asked her to forget about it and just move on. She said, "No." We argued, and I pushed her too hard. Her head hit the cement, and she died instantly.

I couldn't deal with what I had done. I ran up the steps and wrote myself a letter from Mama telling Dawn and me that she had to leave. I put the letter under my pillow, and I kept that story alive in my mind. That way, Mama would never be dead; she had just left for the market. The only problem was Mama's death stopped me from functioning. I could've killed a hundred more people before I got caught, but mothers are special.

When Mama died, I died too. I could no longer strategically move. I went so crazy that I stayed in that stinking-ass house with two dead bodies because I was afraid of reality. Mama was the reason I got caught. In some sick way, I didn't want to leave her.

Dr. Smidget was an idiot. I played with him all the time, just to get more drugs, just to escape my true reality.

"I told you when *you* leave, *they* leave," Crazy Joe said. "What goes up must come down. I told you, I fucking told you. We are on a foreign planet."

"Crazy Joe, don't start that dumb-ass foreign planet junk," I said as I got up to brush my teeth. "I had a long night, and I'm not in the mood for your looney talk or none of that crazy shit."

"Crazy shit for Crazy Joe. Crazy shit for Crazy Joe. And you calling *me* crazy? You killed your entire family, tough guy. I should call you Crazy Damien, but it doesn't sound as good. You don't know nothing about what goes up, and you damn sure don't know about what goes down. That's why you are stuck!"

Crazy Joe took out his notebook and repeatedly wrote the words *crazy shit for crazy joe*.

I began brushing my hair. "Oh, you want to talk about what I did? Do you remember how *you* got in here, Crazy Joe? Do you? Nevermind. I don't have time to talk to you today. I have a date with Emma."

"You don't have no damn date with Emma. You have nothing, absolutely nothing. Until you realize we are on a foreign planet, you will have nothing, and you won't be nothing."

"I'm something. Everyone sees me, and you are just jealous that I have a date with Emma. When was the last time someone came to talk to you?"

"Yesterday. Yup, yesterday, not today or tomorrow, but yesterday. I know my shit. You just be blacking out, so you never see me talk to Emma, but I did yesterday. It's not a date. Emma doesn't even like you! Don't nobody like you, Damien, not even your imaginary sister."

"I don't like none of you either, not even Emma.

My real date is with Craig, and Emma is just the way Craig and I can see each other discreetly. Anyway, mind your own business and get out of my way."

"Don't tell me what to do! I will whip your ass worse than Big Mike did. He had you rolling around on the floor calling your mama. I know what goes up must come down, so nobody tries to whip my ass. I'll tell you that! I'll tell you that today, not yesterday, but today. You feel me?" Crazy Joe's eyes were dead serious.

"Nope! Don't know what you are talking about today or yesterday."

Crazy Joe continued to talk, but I ignored his nonsense. I was relieved when I heard Emma's cheap high-heeled shoes clicking down the hall. Emma thought she could fix me. She believed she was the master of counseling. I played with her mind every session like an old raggedy doll. Sometimes I thought about just wringing her skinny, wrinkled neck. I wanted her to shut up, the same way I wanted Crazy Joe to shut up, the same way I had wanted Brianna to shut up.

Brianna had had the nerve to say I raped her. She had wanted it, maybe not as rough as I gave it to her, but she had wanted it. I choked her to death with my bare hands to shut her up. I then dipped my penis in her corpse as she sat there lifeless and dead. Her mouth was still warm as I slowly stuck my penis in and out until I released all my energy all over her face. It was the most exhilarating thing I'd ever experienced.

Emma was getting close. I could feel she was about to open the door at any moment. I was sure she'd have on a pencil skirt with a white blouse, and she'd be ready to talk to me with a shaky tone as if walking on eggshells. She was always afraid I'd get upset, and that scared the shit out of her. She talked to me like I was a child, and I hated it. I hated fear. I wished she would grow some balls and just speak to me. Emma wanted to know what went on in my mind, and if she stopped being a pussy and talked to me straight, I'd tell her.

Craig escorted me to her office with his buff arms. He stayed there for every session to ensure I didn't attack anyone.

Emma had the typical therapist's office. There was a long chair for the patients, a stiff chair for her to sit on, some stupid plants, and a few books on the bookshelves. God, everyone was so fucking ordinary. It made me sick. Every time I set foot in her office, I wanted to kill her and rid the world of her ordinariness. She couldn't be happy, pretending to be like the others.

Today was the day I would look in the mirror. I

hadn't looked in one since Mama died—it was too painful.

"Damien, how are you feeling?" Emma asked in a low, pitying tone.

"Emma, how are *you* feeling?" I mocked. "Do you hear how that sounds? Would you want someone to talk to you like you're a three-year-old?"

"No, Damien. How would you like me to talk to you?"

"Regular! I've decided to open up this session, and I will actually tell you some things, but only if you can be real."

Emma raised an eyebrow. "How would you like me to be? What is real?"

"I would like you to be yourself. Talk to me like a friend, not all that therapist stuff."

I sat down in the chair instead of on the sofa. "Before we get started, you must do two things."

"You know that's my spot, Damien. Please sit where you should sit."

"I'm tired of sitting there, and I would like to sit here for this session. Are you going to do the two things?" I kept my back ramrod straight, like a true professional.

"Okay, Damien. I'll sit in the patient's chair," Emma replied as she sat down, shifting uncomfortably. "What are the two things?"

"You made a good decision by playing along. The first thing I need you to do is unbutton the top three buttons of your shirt—not to your breast, but enough that it's not buttoned up to your neck. It annoys me, and I hate that you are so typical. The second thing is to take off those cheap-ass shoes. Just let your feet feel the carpet, or your stockings or whatever." I pointed at her feet.

"Emma, you don't have to do that!" Craig, standing guard at the door, blurted.

"It's okay, Craig. I'll play along. If Damien is going to be honest this session, what're a few buttons and a pair of shoes that are killing my feet anyway?" she slightly joked as she unbuttoned her blouse and kicked her heels to the side.

"Very good," I said. "This is the most authentic I've ever seen you. How do you feel?"

"I feel well. Now let's get started. Can we talk about Mama today?"

"No!"

"I thought you were ready to open up." She sounded disappointed. "Okay, can we talk about Dawn then?"

"What do you want to know?"

Emma squirmed on the sofa, trying to get comfortable. "Why do you think she's alive? Why do you blame her for everything?"

"Dawn is very much alive. Twins are special. So to the world, Dawn died at birth, but she didn't really. She left her body and jumped into mines. Dawn is the real monster. You have no idea what she's capable of. I can't always control her." I lowered my head.

"How long were you aware of Dawn being a part of you?" she asked while writing something on her notepad.

"As long as I could remember. It started off small. Dawn would knock things out of my hands and tell me to hit my friends. That was just the beginning."

Emma looked directly into my eyes. "How do you know it was Dawn and not an unwanted voice in your head? We all have voices and thoughts in our minds."

"She's not a voice, though. *You* can't see her, but *I* can see her clearly. Right now, she is sitting next to you. She is actually upset that I'm talking with you. She told me multiple times not to talk about her in therapy."

"So, she's sitting right here?" Emma pointed to her right.

"No, she's on the other side." I pointed.

"Are you afraid of Dawn?" Emma asked, avoiding looking to her other side.

"No, but you should be. Dawn can't hurt me

physically, or it would hurt her too. She can only hurt me mentally by doing things to the people I love. Like Mama." I lowered my head again.

"How is it that Dawn is doing these things instead of you?"

"Are you even listening?" I answered, frustrated. "She is alive and can do what she wants. Sometimes, she takes over my body when I'm asleep. She decides, and I can't control her!"

"I've always seen you as strong and intelligent. You mean to tell me you can't control your dead twin sister?" She raised her eyebrows.

"No, I can't. Dawn has been with me since birth, and I love her. We are stuck together, and although I get pissed at her actions, she is me, and I am her."

"You don't think she is just your imaginary friend and an excuse for you to keep doing horrible things? It conveniently allows you to blame someone else. You never have to face it?"

Emma tried to button up one of her buttons while I wasn't looking.

"Leave your shirt alone, or I will leave the session. No, Dawn is not an imaginary friend. She's real; Brianna knows she's real." Emma was starting to agitate me, and she knew it.

Emma's pencil scratched at the paper. "Tell me about Brianna. Was she your best friend or Dawn's?"

"She was Dawn's best friend, but she had a crush on me. Brianna was charming and sweet. Dawn mentally tortured her from the very beginning." I shook my head.

"So it was Dawn who raped and killed her? Not you?"

I crossed my arms. "I never said I was innocent, Emma. I did have rough sex with her, but I wouldn't call it rape; she willingly came to the park with me that night. I didn't kidnap her and drag her there."

"Well, who killed her?" Emma asked.

"Dawn killed her. I did have oral sex with her corpse after, but I didn't actually kill any of them. Dawn is the killer. I do things, but I let them live. Dawn has a temper, and so she kills everyone."

"Damien, I have to be honest. I think it works in your favor to blame everything on Dawn."

"Think about this, Emma. If I was the killer, wouldn't I have killed Papa? I hate him the most, but Dawn loves him. Papa is her weakness, and she would never hurt him. *I* would, though. I don't love Papa at all. He's a no-good cheating drunk."

"So, Damien, what if you do love Papa? What if you love him the most, which is why you didn't kill him? How do you know what's true or not? Are you sure you would kill your father?" Emma's pencil moved at a frantic pace. Her voice sounded distracted, confused, as if she were having trouble keeping up.

"The question should be," I countered, "how do you know what's true or not? Do you know who *you* really are?"

"Of course I do," Emma answered, "but this is not about me."

"It's not about me, either. I don't think you know who you are. We all play different characters, Emma. You fake a lot. I see you change your tone of voice when Dr. Smidget comes around; you turn into an ass-kisser, and that's a character. I see how you joke with Craig and try to be cool with the other staff, and that's a character. Then you get serious with the patients and ask all these dumb-ass questions, and that's a character. But you don't know who you are."

I smirked. "Look at you sitting there uncomfortable because your blouse is unbuttoned and your shoes are off. You are probably fearful someone will see you and think you are being unprofessional."

"Okay, so now I'm the patient?" she asked, loosening herself up by wiggling her shoulders.

"Of course not," I said, sitting up straight again in Emma's rigid chair. "I'm just establishing that you clearly don't know what's true or not."

"Thanks for pointing that out and thanks for

opening up about Brianna. That's the most we've ever talked about her. I would like to ask about Mama today. All the years you've been here, and you never said one sentence about your mother. Talking about her will really help your progress."

I frowned. "There you go! You always go too far. Okay, let's talk, but first, you must unbutton another button and slip off your stockings. They have a run on your right leg, and it's unflattering."

"Mrs. Emma, you don't have to do that," Craig insisted. "Damien, you are going too far now."

I glared at Craig. "Too far? Yeah, like how far I stuck my dick down your throat? I thought therapy was supposed to be private, anyway?"

"Your fucking—" Craig started to yell before Emma cut him off.

"Damien, Dr. Smidget ordered that no one is to be left alone with you," she said. "Focus on us, never mind Craig. At the beginning of the session, you said I only had to do two things. You are not keeping your word, Damien." She glanced at her ripped pantyhose.

"I also said I wouldn't talk about Mama. You said okay, and now *you* are not keeping your word."

"See, Damien; if I unbutton one more button, I will be showing cleavage, and that's unprofessional. The stockings can go—I agree they are not very flattering."

"The button or nothing. Just rip off the stockings and stop overthinking. Besides, according to everyone here, I'm gay. I'm not into your cleavage. I want you to be as uncomfortable as you are making me. Now let's talk." I gestured for her to get a move on.

"This is ridiculous," she said as she tore her stockings and unbuttoned the next button, revealing the crease line of her breasts.

"Great! Now that you look like a whore, we can talk," I laughed. "Mama was a fox. She always smelled good, and she was the definition of black beauty. She had thick natural hair, not like that fake stuff you are wearing. I was completely obsessed with Mama's hair. She should've been a chef. She cooked better than anyone I've ever met to this day."

I smiled. "Oh, and her hugs. They were the best! She would hug you tight and rub your back. It was so comforting. But—" I stopped mid-sentence.

Emma's eyes were bright with curiosity. "But, what? Please continue."

"But she was weak. Kind of like you. Mama wanted to be accepted by everyone, especially Papa. She also bitched a lot."

Emma leaned back, offended. "You think I'm weak? What do you mean by accepted? Why do you keep comparing me to your mother?"

"Yes, you are weak. Even weaker than Mama. You are nothing like Mama, so don't think I'm comparing. My mother was gorgeous, and you are average at best. The only similarity is you both wanted acceptance. You can't just be yourself."

I picked up the glass container and poured myself a glass of water.

Emma crossed her arms. "I disagree. You don't know me at all, Damien."

"I thought this was about me, not you." I raised the glass container. "Water?"

"No, thanks. Please continue."

"Mama was smart, but she sometimes did stupid things. It really pissed me off. Like one time, she was under the bed praying as if Dawn couldn't get to her under the bed. We just watched her and laughed. Dawn was a little jealous of Mama, you know?"

"Really? Why would you be jealous of your mother—I mean, why would Dawn be?"

"Dawn wanted all of Papa's attention, and she didn't like it when Mama was around. But I better stop talking about that because Dawn is getting upset. I would hate for her to hurt you."

"Hurt me? I'm not afraid of Dawn, Damien."

"Well, you should be." I laughed. "Dawn will kill you and think nothing of it. Oh, you think you are safe? Is that it? I know you don't think Craig's weak-ass could save you. If Dawn really wanted to take your breath right now, you'd be dead, Emma." I laughed again.

"Remember, this is not about me. I'm just telling you I'm not afraid of Dawn, that's all."

"Right, let's get back to Mama. She didn't know how to let shit go. She saw Dawn leave Mr. Ralph's the night of the fire. I told her not to push it, but she wouldn't listen."

"I've often heard you say, 'Mama talked to Dawn.' Did Mama acknowledge Dawn?"

"Dawn is always around. I've heard Mama tell her to do things, but she was talking to me. She's only addressed me as Damien, but certain things I knew she was saying to Dawn."

"So, why did you kill your mother?" Emma bluntly asked.

"Who said I killed her? That's enough about Mama. You are starting to piss me off! Every time I try to trust one of you bitches, here comes the bullshit. You don't ask somebody some shit like that, especially when they are trying to open up."

I rose to leave. "Never mind, fuck this."

"Damien, wait. Please wait. Calm down. I'm so sorry. That was extremely rude of me. Please sit down, and let's just start fresh."

"I love to hear you beg. Look at you. You are

looking more and more like a hooker as the minutes go by. Sitting there, barefoot, with your unshaved legs, unbuttoned blouse, pleading for bad 'ole Damien to have a seat. You are truly a pathetic individual, Emma."

I sat back in her chair, then crossed my legs and waited for her response. Fear was written all over her face.

"Damien, I noticed you love insulting women. Does that make you feel good?"

I poured myself another glass of water. "I only insult the weak ones. Are you offended?"

"No. Just curious. So if we can't talk about Mama, can we at least talk about your Aunt Sheryl?"

"Ugh, this is getting so boring. I won't waste energy on Sheryl. There's no story there. She was a fat, stinking-ass, pissy excuse of a human, and she didn't deserve to breathe this air. We did the world a favor. Trust me."

"So, was it you who killed her or Dawn?" Emma asked while writing in her notepad, never looking up.

"Maybe you are slow—you know, mentally retarded or straight from the short bus. That's what Papa called people like you. What are you not getting? I am Dawn, and Dawn is me. I am evil, and that I will admit, but Dawn is the killer!"

"No, Damien. I don't think I'm retarded. I

finished top in my class. I just wanted to be sure I understood what roles you played."

She sighed. "Okay, let's switch it up. Every session, you mention another victim that we don't know about. Do you care to share today?"

"I guess I can tell you a little bit. First, I want a soda. Can Craig go get it?"

Emma set her notepad and pencil beside her on the sofa. "You know Craig can't leave the room. I can't get you a soda, but will apple juice do?"

"I guess. You always want something from me, but it's hard to get anything from you."

"I'm sorry, Damien," Emma said as she walked to her mini-refrigerator and took out a small apple juice.

I snuck a pen off her desk to use later. I quickly put it in my pocket. She put the juice on the table next to me instead of handing it to me.

"Please continue with your latest victim," she stated as she sat back down and picked up her pencil and notepad.

"Damn, can I finish my juice first?" I rudely asked.

"I'm sorry. I know you mentioned a lady named Vanessa during your blackout. Is she your latest victim?"

"No. I was bored with my imagination, and I made Vanessa up. I've never met her. When I go on these dark blackouts in my mind, anyone can be anybody. Vanessa was pure fiction, but boy did I enjoy torturing her in my mind."

I drank the apple juice in one long series of gulps. "But back to your question: My latest victim was a man, and he deserved it."

"Is it a man you know or a complete stranger?"

"I have no interest in strangers; they are nobodies to me. That's why in reality, Vanessa wouldn't have been an option. Yes, I did know the victim, as you call him. He was pathetic, and I hated looking at him. I'll give you a hint, though, he played a major role in my childhood."

"Major role in your childhood? Like a preacher or something? Did you or your Dawn version of yourself kill him?"

"*I* killed him!" I yelled with confidence.

"I'm confused. I thought you said you were evil, but Dawn was the killer. Why did you kill this particular person?" Emma's pencil scratched violently at the notepad.

"He deserved it. Mama didn't. Brianna didn't. Dawn kills anyone, but I only kill the people who deserve it. I have a heart, you know."

"Yes, I know. How old were you when this person was murdered?"

"Hmmm. Maybe I'm giving you too much. Yeah,

I think I said enough. I'm done with this. Come on, Craig, take me to my room, you big dick, strong arms, sexy motherfucker." I licked my lips.

"Okay, Damien, I think that is enough for today as well," Emma said as she slid her right foot back into her shoe. "Maybe next week we can get more accomplished to help your treatment. I'm super proud of you for opening up today, though."

"Dawn told me to tell you that we won't be having a session next week."

"And why is that?" Emma asked, buttoning her shirt back up to her neck.

"She said we won't be here," I whispered, covering my lips with my fingers.

Epilogue

To you,

Yes, you! Yeah, I'm talking to you, the one who is reading these words right now. Are you disappointed? Did you hope I could be a better person? Did you want Dawn to really exist so I could be the victim? I mean, she does exist, but not in your world. She lives in my world, and that's where you've been; you've been trapped in my world. You've been consumed in my mind and my thoughts. I hope at some point you wanted me to win, you wanted me to be innocent, you wanted me to be free. I want to be free of this mind, too.

You get to leave and go on with your day-to-day life. I'm stuck here with this terrorizing brain. I can feel you are about to leave me soon. I think our time is coming to an end. That pisses me off. I know I can't keep you stuck in my mind forever. If you made it this far, I've had you long enough. I hope you know I do regret killing Mama. She's the only person who ever loved me. I would be lying if I told you I regret anything else. I'm a little disappointed I'm in this hell hole of a psych hospital; I'm even more disappointed that I never left. I've been here since I was sixteen. What a waste of a life. There's so much more I wanted to do.

Are you listening? I hope you are listening because, as you know, I hate to be ignored. Please pay attention; I'll only say this once. If you wander off, you might miss it. I'm praying I get to keep the thrill of stabbing my latest victim in my mind for as long as possible. I keep repeating the act and wishing I had longer. I wanted to see him suffer for every bad thing he'd ever done. Every time I stabbed the knife into the meat of his body, I smiled inside. The blade hitting his skin was tough; I thought it wouldn't puncture him, but once it did, the sensation rippled through my body. I felt every scream in my back, and it almost felt like an orgasm.

I know this is hard to comprehend. You've been in my mind for hours. Following along with a story that doesn't exist. How fucked up is that?

Do you want me to explain? I can't. I can't give you that much power. Don't judge me. At this point, you are choosing to be lost in my mind, and I thank you. I need your company. I'm stuck here, but you're not. But please don't go until we finish this, once and for all.

Okay, I know what you came for. You want answers. You want some closure. You are just like the others. You are always looking for something. Aunt Sheryl was looking for something when I threw her big ass down the steps. They were wrong; her neck didn't break from the fall. I broke her neck after I tortured her stinking ass for weeks. She wanted to fuck little boys because she was nasty and lonely. Can you believe she tried to make me suck her breast? Yuck, just the thought makes me want to vomit.

Speaking of perverts, let's discuss that pink- and brown-lipped freak! Mr. Ralph. Well, I guess if I was Dawn all *along, that would mean he tried to stick his nasty hands up my shorts. Needless to say, the way I butchered his ass, he'll never bother another little boy again. I'm sorry there was no Brandon or Craig. Mr. Ralph didn't have any children. It was all an illusion.*

The truth is I've never been with a man. I've only ever been with Brianna. So I don't even know if I'm gay. I don't know shit. I do think I want my nurse Craig to do something to me, but often I think I just want to kill him. He's always walking around the hospital smiling with his big white teeth. I'm infatuated with Craig. I'm not sure why, but I know I want him somehow. Brandon was the old nurse who worked here when I first arrived. He quit. He couldn't handle my constant sexual harassment. What a pussy!

Speaking of pussy, I often think of it. It's gutty and warm. I want to be in it, just to tear it up. I want to pound the fuck out of it until the woman screams. I'm not interested in pleasurable screams; I only want to hear painful screams.

Does that make me not gay? Should I be labeled at all? What if I just wake up and do whatever I want? Oh, that makes me insane. I think most of you are insane. Most of you are boring, judgmental little fakers. Yeah, I said it. But who am I? The hell if I know. All I know for sure is I'm a murderer (some call me a serial killer), and that's my true secret. That's all I truly know.

Brianna was such a shame. I tried to give her a good comeback in my mind. I tried to make her tuff, beautiful, and a true badass. I wanted to feel how she would feel if she got to see adulthood. Sadly, I robbed her of that. I wanted her to be bitter and angry. I thought she deserved a lavish life, if nothing else. Her parents always had the fanciest things in our neighborhood. I figured she would grow up with champagne taste. We'll never know what she could or could not have been like, since she died in the fire.

I killed her because the thought of what had happened between us made me sick. By giving her my virginity, I gave her a piece of me. She was my second kill after Mr. Ralph. She was just a casualty.

I appreciate you spending this time with me. It's more attention than I ever received in my entire life. I would love to keep chatting, but our time is coming to an end. Maybe I'll see you around. If not, always remember: The truth is within the eyes.

Speaking of eyes, I'm about to close mines forever. I've heard that if you commit suicide, you will go to hell. Well, in my case, that's where I'd be going anyway. I'd rather leave this mediocre life on my terms than let life kill me. If none of those assholes killed me, why would I let life? I surely don't want to grow old and die in this hellhole with these crazy motherfuckers.

Thanks for letting me leave this suicide letter with you. After all, I don't have any family to address it to since I killed them all, except Papa. If you wondered why I let Papa live, I had no choice. He was in jail, and when he was released, I had already been sent to the nut hospital.

My eyes are getting weak as I pop this last pill. I'm glad my final moments were with you. No matter where you are, on a couch, at work, on your bed, or even on an airplane, you are with me at this moment, my last moment. I'm incredibly drowsy now, and it's safe to say my time here is over. I know you will miss me, but don't worry, I'll see you on the dark side.

Yours Truly,
Damien

"In other news, today we received the most disturbing information regarding a homicide. This story hits home to many people in the Detroit community. We finally found the missing Principal, Robert Lewis from Dobson Middle School. His remains were recovered from a house that had been abandoned. Crime scene detectives seem to believe his body suffered multiple stab wounds. According to the coroner's office, he died around the day he went missing about seven years ago. The community was really hoping for his safe return home.

The current students at Dobson Middle School are holding a candlelight vigil tonight. The Detroit Police Department is asking anyone with any information to please come forward."

BOOKS FROM THE AUTHOR

- DAMAGED little girl
- Niña Dañada (spanish version)
- A DAMAGED WOMAN
- DAMIEN'S SECRET
- DAMIEN'S SECRET II

STAY IN CONTACT

- Website: www.naturallysunni.com
- Email: naturallysunnibooks@gmail.com
- Instagram: Sunni_theauthor
- Facebook: Sunni T. Connor
- YouTube: Naturally Sunni